The Dead Shall Rise

THE DEAD SHALL RISE

A TALE OF THE MOUNTAINS

Melanie K. Hutsell

CELTIC CAT PUBLISHING
KNOXVILLE, TENNESSEE
2016

Printed in the United States of America
22 21 20 19 18 17 16   1 2 3 4 5 6 7 8 9 10
ISBN-13: 978-0-9905945-7-4 (paper)

Hutsell, Melanie K.—
    The Dead Shall Rise: A Tale of the Mountains / Melanie K. Hutsell
    ISBN 978-0-9905945-7-4

Celtic Cat Publishing
Knoxville, Tennessee
CelticCatPublishing.com

The Dead Shall Rise

FALL

I

She came from the lowlands, her long, black hair wild and tangled as blackberry thickets. She came alone, and she walked with sorrow in her long bones. The people of Beulah Creek had never seen anyone like her. They did not want to see her. They knew it that first morning when she walked into their midst. She seemed to clutch the dark about her like the long folds of her skirt, the fringes of her shawl. When she passed, people were unsettled by her presence as they might be by a half-remembered dream or by the sliver of moon seen through the last, rasping leaves of autumn.

For days, weeks after, the Beulah Creek dwellers told of her across fences, shared stories of her around the dinner table or the television. More than one old woman shook her head and declared the stranger a tormented soul. It was because of her eyes, Veeny Anderson explained. They made Veeny cold all over, shivery and shaky and just plain wrong, when the stranger woman looked at her with the huge, black, haunted eyes that seemed to see so far away, as though the woman looked out across the land beyond the mountains, all the way to the ocean and the sands of North Carolina. And those who heard Veeny were inclined to agree. It was most unnatural, the strange, mournful brightness of the woman's black eyes.

And yet in many ways the stranger woman had seemed earthly enough, a tall, plain creature, who carried herself with a rugged sort of elegance. She came in early September in the year 2000, walking up the road. She wore something about her neck, some sort of pendant, which she fingered and grasped often as she looked about her, at the maple trees and the holly bushes and the old bungalows. She smiled at the twin Mullins girls eating apples and rocking in the old green glider on their concrete porch. Her smile touched her lips, but never moved any other part of her face. Kenny McGuire's hound began to bark and moan, and people began to notice. She walked up to Jack Hendrick's gas and grocery by the Beulah Creek Baptist Church.

Jack remembered he was taking some Windex to the front door when the woman was suddenly standing there on the other side of the glass. He jumped, knocking the door so that the bells jangled on their ropes.

"Morning," he finally managed to say, and he pushed on the door to crack it open, to invite her inside. "Can I help you with something, ma'am?"

The woman nodded. "Please," she said. Jack tried not to wince at her strange, hoarse voice. "I'm looking for a place."

She said the word as though it meant something very special. He thought it an odd thing to say.

"Whereabouts? You know the name of it?" he asked her.

She shook her head. "I don't know what place it might be. I thought I might find it here. I sold my car down the road a ways."

For all her strange clothes, her weird eyes, and her rasping, hissing voice, Jack could tell that she did not talk like a stranger, as though she belonged someplace close by.

"It was such a beautiful day driving," she continued, "and I could smell the trees and the sun as I was driving along, with my windows down. I felt like a walk, to see if I might not have found it. Is there someplace around here, empty?"

Jack frowned, his brows drawing together. "You mean a house or something?"

"Yes." Her long, bony fingers wrapped around the pendant. "I want to live."

His skin began to crawl and squirm like earthworms then. "There's no houses," he stammered, "not here. Least none you'd want to live in, falling down and full of rattlesnakes like the old Greenberry place."

"Do they live there?" she asked. "The Greenberrys?"

Jack let drop his hand with the Windex bottle. He felt a sag in his shoulders. "Not anymore. They're all buried up top of the hill, Sumac Hill there behind the house, except for Ruth, and she's in the church graveyard. I reckon . . . I reckon Clement Foster is the one you'd want to talk to, if you want to see about that house."

She tilted her head forward, once. "Thank you."

As she turned to go, the shawl swinging about her shoulders to the sway of her long black hair, Jack watched the way she walked, the sudden, furtive movement of her joints. He remembered the shadows of deer he had seen deep in the woods. He heard himself call after her, "Clement won't be home until late. He works down at the plant in Millsborough. Why don't you go up the road to mine and Judy's place? She'll be there. You can sit awhile until supper time."

The woman turned back, that sad smile wandering across her lips. "I'll just walk around, I think."

And so it was, some time later, that Emmy Foster was sitting out on the porch when the stranger woman walked up the long slope to the house. The windchimes sang out the notes the wind carried. Emmy twisted a long, fine lock of reddish hair about her finger as she looked at her Bible and put her hands upon the words. Nobody in Beulah Creek could have named a thought in her head. She was a vegetable sort of girl, dewy-eyed and mild as daisies, her lips budding sweetly in a creamy face. Yet she was thick like her father, her hands made of bread, her new breasts broad and sturdy for such a sun-skimming child as she.

The first thing she knew of the woman was when she heard a ragged voice say, "Hello."

Emmy lifted her head and looked right into that woman's face. She had no breath left to speak Jesus's name. The dark face before her was the holiest she had ever known. The woman's eyes were wrought of cataclysm, of the heavens cracking apart. Emmy had dreamed it in the hard pews. The hollows of it had come to her as she prayed on an Easter morning. She sat up very straight on the edge of the rocking chair.

"Yes, ma'am. I know who you are," Emmy said. "You're Mary Magdalene."

The woman turned up her mouth wearily. "Do you think so?"

Emmy moved the palm of her hand upon the paper. "I've learned you all my life," she said. Her heart began to flutter like a butterfly in the summer flowers. "Did you come here on purpose? Would you tell me what that's like, to be Mary Magdalene?" She wondered at the beauty and the shining of Jesus rising in the most glorious magenta of all. She looked at the pendant hanging around the woman's neck, a cross in a circle, but not quite, Emmy realized. The two cross pieces crossed right in the center. "I'm Emmy Foster," she said. "My daddy isn't here right now."

"I was walking," the woman said. "I wanted to see the Greenberry house."

"Nobody wants to see it," said Emmy, frowning. She closed the book in her lap. "Jess Greenberry died there, she's my mama's great-aunt. She walks sometimes at night."

"I could keep her company, then."

Emmy shivered. "Are you a ghost, too?" The woman kept fear in that silver circle, held as with a magnet, bound as with a chain.

"I'm alive and mean to remain so. I've known ghosts enough." The woman's face was long and sad and silent. "You can call me Malathy Joan."

"Is that what you'd rather?" Emmy hardly dared to breathe. It was a name to whisper, a name of sacred shadows, a name of steely, glinting armor. She heard it and saw a wounded face of glowing embers beneath the night sky of October.

"It's what's best, I think," said the stranger woman who called herself Malathy Joan.

Emmy did not know if it were best, but it was beautiful, and she would speak it as she was told. She ran her fingers across the comfortable cracks and worn places of her Bible cover. She liked the feeling it gave her heart. "Can I get you something? Daddy got us a box of those little cheese crackers, I hadn't opened them yet. They're good with some grape juice or some Coke."

Malathy Joan shifted her head. There were golden flecks in her eyes that leaped suddenly bright. "I'd like to walk up and see the Greenberry house. Would you take me?"

Emmy stood, and the rocker creaked. She had never felt so big inside. She placed her Bible in the seat. "Yes, ma'am. I'll get us some Cokes to take." The windchimes stirred, striking two notes again and again. It was the trembling pulse at her wrists. She wanted to stay with this Mary Magdalene, who wore fear about her neck on a silver chain and stayed alive. This was wonderful to her, more than anything she ever imagined. She had always loved this woman, dark and irresistible and serene. Malathy Joan came from long ago and would go there again, wrapping it about her as she wrapped the shawl about her shoulders. Emmy would go after her always.

In the days that followed, many in Beulah Creek shook their heads and said that the olive-skinned stranger woman had a familiar spirit indeed to so quickly capture the slow, shy heart of Emmy Foster. But Emmy herself had only delighted in that afternoon, singing softly as she and Malathy Joan toiled through the long grass and up the long slope to the Greenberry place. She drank the sweetness out of the aluminum can and watched the grass fall before them, swaying, nodding in the breeze. The dark-clothed woman said nothing, except once Emmy heard her murmur, as though chanting a prayer, "I think I could live here."

"There's plenty folks do their living at Beulah Creek," Emmy said, brushing the delicate chestnut curls of her hair from before her eyes.

The woman's long face made Emmy think of the lonesome darkness that clustered down in the creek bottom on winter nights.

"I came to find things," said Malathy Joan. "Things that aren't just anywhere. I came to lose the world out there."

Emmy watched the pendant swing against the woman's flat chest. "That house up there," she said, "done lost everything it ever had. Except Jess Greenberry, I reckon."

They could see the Greenberry place now. Malathy Joan stiffened a little in her walk, and then began to walk faster. Her legs were long, and her strides were quick and fervent. Emmy struggled to keep pace with her. Then suddenly Malathy Joan stopped.

"It's like I've seen this," she whispered. "I don't understand."

It was a skull of a house, its eyesockets hollow. But it was not quite dead, only wearing away beneath the years. The old boards were wound about and covered over with honeysuckle and wisteria. The front door gaped an uneasy welcome. Malathy's arm hung heavy at her side, her fingers open. Her other hand tugged at the bit of metal on its chain around her neck.

"Is there a carpenter in town?" she asked.

"There's Noah," gasped Emmy. She panted to snatch her breath back, looking up at the sky a well-worn blue. It seemed so close here, like she could reach up and touch it. The proud, tall chimney held it off of her and the stranger woman, and then Sumac Hill reared up behind the house, pressing itself against the topmost sky. Emmy liked the deep cranberry color of sumac, tucked inside her.

Malathy Joan was nodding slowly. "That's it, then." She turned about, her long, dark hair catching the wind. "I'm not going anywhere else." The fringe of her shawl ruffled like the grass.

Emmy felt many bright bubbles rising inside her, surging. "I'll be so glad to keep you, Malathy Joan," she said. Her hand was slick from the sweating can. She reached for the gentle tufts of the woman's shawl, and they tickled her palm like cat's fur. Emmy could not stop her face from gladness. "Please come on down and sit awhile until Daddy comes home."

And so that evening, when Clement Foster got out of his truck, he looked up to the front porch, where his daughter would be waiting. Supper would be simmering in the slow cooker where he had left it that morning, and the house would be warm. It was a comfortable thought to him, as the sky dimmed a soft, gentle purple, and the air turned cool.

He took a few steps toward the porch and then stopped, unable to move, but just as alarmed to stand there and see the figure sitting in his rocking chair, lilting back and forth.

"My Lord," he whispered. All the years he had lived in this house, he had been afraid to know the truth, to know what walked high on the hill where his wife's kin had lived and where their bones rested now.

The rocking chair slowed, creaked into silence. "Are you Clement Foster?"

"Yes, ma'am," he said, faltering, stumbling nearer. "Did you want something with me?" His palms turned damp.

"I'm wanting to buy the Greenberry place. I was told to speak with you."

He stopped again. "I don't reckon we're acquainted."

"You can call me Malathy Joan."

Clement could not see her face. He could only see her long hair, her long skirts, and hear her croaking voice. "You're not . . . you're not her?" he said. "Come down here?"

There was a pause. "I'm myself, is all," the strange voice replied.

The front door jerked open. Emmy stood there, her sturdy body framed in the light from the kitchen. The front room was dark.

"Hi, Daddy," she said. "I told her about Noah and maybe she could stay here awhile."

He stood and looked at the shape of his daughter. It seemed incredible to him that the presence of the stranger woman in the rocking chair did not dismay her. He knew Emmy shrank to his side and clung to his hand when they passed noisy, eager dogs or even regular folks in the town.

Emmy stiffened. "You're going to sell it, ain't you, Daddy?"

Clement came up the steps then. He could hear the sound of his feet solid against the concrete. The sound steadied him. It was very, very real, the sound and feel of concrete. He came towards the dark place where the woman's voice was. His heart was thundering through the mountains as he leaned near, peering at her, and said, "Ma'am, I don't mean disrespect, but I'm going to ask you this anyhow. Tell me you're a living, breathing woman and not Mrs. Greenberry come back."

The head turned to look at him. Clement could just glimpse one huge, dark eye, glittering in the light from the door.

"I'm not dead," said the ragged voice of the stranger woman. "I promise you."

"Well, that's all right, then," he said, still uncertain.

He put out his hand. She lifted her own hand, and her fingers slipped smooth and gentle about his fingers, clasping them. He was startled. Her bones were so long, so thin, he felt he would break them if he clutched her too harshly. He had not thought she would be so fragile.

There was a shudder in his throat like laughter. "Glad to know you, ma'am. If we're looking to be neighbors, I reckon I ought to be more neighborly."

She moved her head in acceptance. He could barely see her, but he heard the soft moan of the rocking chair.

"I would like a neighbor," she said. "It's been a long time since I lived somewhere."

Hearing the sadness in her, Clement felt how unkindly he had spoken. She was a stranger sitting on his porch, come to speak with him, and her odd way of talking was nothing but reticence. Jess Greenberry might walk Sumac Hill and every room in the old house beneath it, but he could feel the pulse fluttering at Malathy Joan's wrist, her bones delicate as glass. The windchimes stirred with the coming dark.

"You come on in," he said. He heard the front door behind him creak. "Come on and eat you something, you're more than welcome to what there is. We can talk over houses and everything then."

"I'll do that," she said, rising in the dusk.

And that was how the stranger woman came to Beulah Creek in the fall of the year. She shared a meal that night with the Fosters, and a day or two after, Jack Hendrick told Sam and Kenny McGuire that Clement was going to sell the Greenberry place.

By then, the Beulah Creek people arched their eyebrows significantly when the strange words of that woman's name came across any tongue. All who saw her wondered about her, a most unbeautiful woman, and yet she had a handsome nose, and a way of walking, and her hair was copious and black, black as the wildest, thickest forest choked in December darkness. Perhaps, Veeny Anderson suggested, and others in Beulah Creek agreed, perhaps Malathy Joan walked with the spirits. Perhaps she looked into the spirit world with her far-seeing eyes, as she moved like a phantom thing through the town.

But Noah Carpenter only shrugged his shoulders. He listened to them talking and then walked off, kicking the dirt with his boots. He had never even seen the woman. Most of the ones who talked hadn't either, he figured. To him, there was no use in talking about what a body didn't know.

II

Every soul in Beulah Creek had traced the lurid, lingering story of Jess Greenberry in the landscape about them. The lost syllables of it dropped upon the
very stones of the creek. As folks walked and prayed and cooked and slept, the
lore stirred inside them, and they desired and feared to know the whole truth
of the tale. People living there and elsewhere in those mountains regarded the
stories of their ancestors much the same, with trepidation, both venerating and
renouncing, more than half-believing such knowing of the past could render
them captive, could in fact trace the coal and limestone truth of what they
would become.

But among the people of Beulah Creek, only Hazel Barnes had known the
living Jess Greenberry. What was more, she gripped her knowledge as a Mason
jar kept a struggling moth, its wings pounding hideously against the glass. No
one in the town had succeeded in prying the least part from her fingers, and
few had dared even to try.

As a child of eleven, Hazel had witnessed Jess's coffin go in the ground. As a
young woman, Hazel had watched death like a green, mandibled mantis that
flapped about the sick rooms of Beulah Creek. Long years ago, children took
these words whispered from behind their elders' hands to trade for frogs and
marbles among themselves. Long years ago, the children had grown, but they
believed the words about Grandma Barnes as they believed in God. They kept
their careful distance from her and forgot her, mostly. But her house sat snug
and tidy beneath the gnarled apple boughs when they passed it, and her small
yard sparkled in the rain, nursing a penchant for wild strawberries.

She was summoned still when a baby struggled for breath or a man broke his leg. Then she came creaking upon her cane with a satchel snagged in her thorny hand, her skin hanging like burlap from her skeleton.

When she thumped up to the sick bed and named the ailment, she snatched out a plastic bag with bits of crushed leaf and wadded it firmly onto the nightstand. Nobody laughed, but always, the Beulah Creek dwellers brewed the leaf or spread the unguent as she told them. She came often to quiet the sick, her hair thin and fluffed like a mad burst of milkweed. But she came seldom, in those latter days, to trap death in her cupped hands as she had done for years and years before, long before Dr. Franklin had set up shopkeeping in Millsborough, down in the lowlands.

Soon after the stranger woman arrived in Beulah Creek, Grandma Barnes walked out her own door in daylight and banged it firmly behind her. She wore her red kerchief pulled over her head and tied under her chin, to keep away the earache, as she took her way through the peppery air. Her cane thumped a marred rhythm upon the earth. She knew that she moved haltingly beneath a dying star, and all about her leaves blighted and curled, as was the way of things. Sometimes she stopped, her chest laboring, and squinted at the run of colors bleeding across her sight.

Behind her came a black dog, a large mongrel. It moved as soundlessly as the old woman's shadow that slipped and pulled along the ground. The creature had no name. She called it dog, and the dog blinked its yellow eyes and often came when she spoke. That morning, Grandma Barnes carried her bones along the road and let the dog follow. She was bound over the creek and up the hill to the Fosters' home to say words at the black-eyed stranger there.

When at last she neared the top of the long, gravel driveway, her cane crunching among the rocks, she saw Malathy Joan sitting in the rocker upon the porch. The dark woman was drinking from a tall glass and watching the leaves drift slowly down the sky. The rocker sat still. Emmy's orange tabby cat sat in the woman's lap and kneaded its paws in the fabric of her long brown skirt. Malathy Joan dropped thin fingers and stroked beneath the animal's chin.

"I hear you come to stay awhile," Grandma Barnes called. It was a penetrating voice that cracked from the stooped, shriveled body. "Hear you're aiming to buy the old Greenberry place and set up house in it."

Malathy Joan lifted her gold-glittering eyes. "Yes," she said. "I mean to stay a good while."

Grandma Barnes stopped at the sound of Malathy's mangled voice. The crunching of gravel hushed.

"My people are from a town like this," said Malathy Joan. She leaned carefully and set the glass beside the rocker. The cat squirmed in her lap. She gathered bony arms under the animal and stood from the rocking chair. The grey shawl about her slipped a little, the fringe stirring. "It will be a good thing, and peaceable to me, I think, to be neighbor to you all." Her hair tumbled down her back and shoulders, heavy as hemlock shadows under spreading boughs.

Grandma Barnes squinted up at her. "Maybe Jess won't let you stay."

"That could be," said Malathy. Her hand paused from caressing the cat. "But I mean it otherwise."

Grandma Barnes stabbed the rocks with her cane. The dog padded to the old woman's side and watched.

"Nobody's took up in that place since Saul and them little ones quit it," said Grandma Barnes. "You can't be going in there and putting it back. It won't go back. Not like you're meaning, all neat and tidy and scrubbed clean of what's been lived in that place."

Malathy held to the cat and looked at Grandma Barnes with eyes like winter fields. "Why would you wish to tell me so?"

"I don't wish nothing, girl. I know things." The old woman's face was loose and crinkled so that it was hard to see her eyes, but there was no ease in the set of her shoulders or the bite of her voice. "If you don't see fit to listen, and go on heedless, then it will all come to nothing, what you do or don't do, or whether I speak or hold my tongue." Grandma Barnes laid her hands flat upon the head of her cane. "You can see far, I don't doubt. Maybe you know a thing or two about the woman that walks that place. But I've come to say there's no cause to be opening up what ought to stay shut." She cupped her hands and straightened. The dog whined, barked once, and was silent again. "Everybody needs a place to go," said Grandma Barnes. "Build you a house with your own two hands and welcome. But don't be bringing trouble down on us by going up there and making your home with it."

The cat that Emmy called Pumpkin wriggled and flailed in the dark woman's arms. The wind chimes jangled in a sudden fit of wind.

"I don't wish to trouble Jess Greenberry or anyone else," said Malathy. "I would be glad to share with her what peace comes to me here." She walked to the Fosters' front door. She turned and opened the screen door, and let Pumpkin dart from her. He leaped and shot away into the living room.

"I don't know as peace ever set foot in that house up the slope," said Grandma Barnes. "Jess was a restless one, willful as the devil. Who can know the mind of such a one?"

Malathy walked to the edge of the porch. The dog looked up at her, its tongue lolling from its mouth. She tugged the grey shawl tighter about her. "What do you know of her? How did she die?"

"She died a miserable death," said Grandma Barnes. She wrenched her face as she spoke. "For Jess was proud and high-spirited, a beautiful, cunning creature, and she lived her life chasing after wind."

The old woman never hesitated, but told Malathy Joan no more than what she had already meant to say. She told nothing of the secrets she herself had witnessed long ago, of the young man who had slipped from the back door of the Greenberry house many a late night or early morning when Saul was away.

"They found Jess hanging," Grandma Barnes said, "and cut her down from the rafters. She died of being Saul Greenberry's wife long before."

Malathy shook her head slightly. The slender, olive fingers touched the pendant on its chain. "I've seen death before." The name she had given over had carried death with it, cold and heavy as iron chains wound all about her body. "I don't fear it as I did once."

The dog sniffed. Grandma Barnes leaned forward. "And I reckon I've beheld it a time or two myself. And when it comes for me, I'll look it straight in the eye and go. But there's no sense in making it your dwelling place before."

Malathy Joan turned the pendant about in her fingers and was silent.

"The world is a haunted place," she said, finally. "And yet there are those who are able to walk through the dark streets and bear grace in their arms. I know it is true." Clutching her shawl close, she said then, "Will you eat something before you go?"

The dog yawned, groaning. Grandma Barnes jabbed her cane into the gravels. "I reckon I've got what I come for. Thank you anyhow." And she jerked away down the hill again.

But Malathy Joan merely clasped the pendant in her fingers and was at peace. There were no more hunks of flesh to be taken from her body, from her heart. It mattered little what words were spoken of her, what darkened corners they shaped for her to inhabit. Already, she felt the living rise up in her, like the stretching, yawning sense that spread to fingertips and toes when sleeping passed slowly into waking. It was not a thing she had known often. She welcomed it in her way.

In the mornings, she came barefoot down the stairs in the Fosters' home. She went into the kitchen, her long hair flowing down her back. She wore clothes that eddied about her, sometimes long, dark skirts, sometimes a smock and loose pants. In the early morning quiet, the house still dim, she broke eggs and put bread into the toaster. Soon, the most wonderful smells would emanate from the stove. This was life to her, the scent of it, the taste of it, the warmth of it. This was work that her hands knew, and it gave her pleasure to make it, to set it upon the table, rich as harvest fields and colorful as autumn mountains.

Those who had taken Malathy Joan into their home were more than pleased to have her. Now when awakening from dreams of the Greenberry house in spring, Emmy Foster stirred and rubbed her eyes, breathing the air hungrily. She lay back on the pillow and watched the wind move through the pale curtains. Emmy knew how to make toast and even heat strips of bacon in the microwave, but she did not know how Malathy Joan wrought those meals. She had never eaten food like it before in her life. It tasted. It always tasted brilliantly, poignantly. It was never burned or underdone, it was never too hot or too cold. Emmy's heart was filled with the wonder of it, and her eyes with the shy smiling thanks for it, every time she approached the table and saw the vase of chrysanthemums on the table, the bowl of sausage gravy, or the basket covered with the blue cloth to keep the biscuits warm.

Emmy's father, Clement, now, too, came down to breakfast a bit more quickly, a bit more eagerly, than before. It was a blessing to be awake for it, he thought. The fragile, long-fingered hand that set the plate of sliced tomatoes and the jar of apple butter upon the table was as real and fleshly as his own, and it was kindly, too. If she was a witch, he said to Jack Hendrick, laughing, she did her witchery in the kitchen, and he for one was glad of what she did. She would make a good neighbor, and he was more than ready to talk a little business with her. It was high time to do so, if the stranger woman meant to live in the Greenberry place before winter began to fall in shivering pieces from the sky.

On a Friday night, a good night for visiting, Clement Foster finally brought Noah Carpenter up to the house. Malathy Joan was in the kitchen, stirring the soup. She wore a long, burgundy dress, her hair unbound, and she hummed a little as she stirred. There were corn muffins in the oven and zinnias in a blue vase on the kitchen table. Pumpkin was weaving in and out of the table legs, his long tail wriggling. Otherwise, the house was still, warm and comfortable in its quiet.

Emmy set the plates down on the table. She stooped and patted Pumpkin's head, then straightened and pulled back the kitchen curtains, looking up the hill to the Greenberry house. The trees on Sumac Hill writhed against the orange, unhallowed sky. It drew her eyes, and she shuddered at the power there.

The front door opened and closed. There were footsteps in the living room, and then Clement was saying, "Shouldn't wonder if we had a right cold one this year."

"Hi, Daddy," called Emmy, letting the curtain fall. She turned back to the table and began setting the plates on the blue placemats. "Hi, Noah," she whispered shyly, knowing she should speak, hoping he would not hear.

Malathy glanced over her shoulder as the two men came into the kitchen. She saw Clement's broad and ruddy face and stocky shoulders, and her lips turned up their smile.

"Malathy, this is Noah Carpenter, he's a long-time friend of mine," said Clement, nodding to her.

Her eyes flicked to the other man's face. Noah was younger than Clement Foster. People in Beulah Creek whispered Noah had a good deal of Indian blood in him, with his raw-boned face, brown skin, and hard, dark eyes. He stood now and looked at her, unflinchingly. Neither did she look away. His response was something far other than fear, she realized, but she could not recognize what it might be. "Hello," she said.

Her voice was rough like unsanded timber. But she herself was tall and straight. There was nothing coarse about her, he could see that at once. He had not thought she would look like this. He did not know what to say, so he said, "Ma'am," and nodded as Clement had done. He was wearing his hat, he realized, then, so he reached up and took it from his head. He clutched it in both hands. Then he thought of something else to say, so he said that also. "Clement tells me you're a mighty good cook."

Her mouth quirked. Her face was somber. "I like to cook." The gold flecks glittered in her eyes. "I know I'm alive then, doing living work. I think it's important, to know yourself alive."

She was a plain woman, no fancy work about her, but Noah admired the way she was made, all the same. Her words were fine things, warm-blooded and sinewed. He thought for a moment. His hands bent his hat back and forth. "The Lord calls us in all kinds of ways. It's always better when we answer, I think."

She tilted her head, once. "I think so, too." It was the best answer she knew, to stand there barefoot in the Fosters' kitchen, high on a hill over Beulah Creek. "How do you usually answer, Noah Carpenter?"

His hands stopped. He swallowed. "I answer real careful, ma'am."

Emmy stood with her arms folded atop the back of the chair. She rested her chin on her arms and wondered if the calling came from the sky, streaming down like glory, strong beams of light that shimmered upon the land. She decided that it would make a warm place inside her that opened like a dewy morning glory. It would be magenta. She liked the word magenta. It was rich and musky. It was the smell of fresh crayons.

"Well, why don't we come on and eat a little and then we'll talk about things," said Clement. "I reckon we're all pretty hungry."

So soup was ladled into bowls, and silverware clinked onto the table. Cold milk was poured into tall glasses and the basket of muffins set next to the vase. But Noah could not remember anything of what he ate when he went home that night. He remembered only that it was warm and good. He ate with his eyes on his bowl and his mind turning and turning about. He did not even know what he was thinking, and then it would come to him, that this woman would take a lot of knowing. Years and years, he thought, the way the rivers dug down, down into the mountains. And then, later, another thing would come, that the people in Beulah Creek were like unlatched gates, always clacking and banging away. It wore him nearly crazy sometimes, how they went on and on. He didn't know how other folks could stand it.

That night when he went home and lay down to sleep, he dreamed that he had gone to look over the Greenberry house, only it was the middle of the night, and the house was a giant thicket of gnarled and tangled darkness. As he stood there, wondering if a moon would rise so he could see, he heard something banging about inside. It was a wild animal, he thought. It knocked against a loose board. He knew it was a wild animal, a rabbit maybe, a deer, but his heart was nearly strangling him, straining into his throat. He stood there, his hands clenched, and waited for the shadow creature to show itself. It never came.

He went around most of the next day thinking how to answer what he saw in his dream. The people of Beulah Creek saw his hard, quiet face and remarked only that Noah Carpenter was morose and unsociable. A good man, they figured, but not one to make conversation. They wondered what would come of him meddling with the Greenberry house. As Veeny Anderson said, tipping her head in the direction of the creek and the high hill beyond, there were some things best let be.

III

The breath of the mountains worn by untold ages formed that morning, drifting from dark slopes upon the September air. It was the land speaking the dead aloud, cold and heavy with memory. The people of Beulah Creek walked to church through the thick vapor while about and above them, hills floated, and trees flickered. Silence fell across the world like steely snow. Old men and their grandsons, hand in hand on their way, covered by the grey clouds of autumn, spun slowly with the world toward the end of all things. It was the day that Malathy Joan at last came down from the Fosters' house to take her place among them.

The congregants of the Beulah Creek Baptist Church greeted one another and murmured together as they stood before the front doors, for the vestibule was too small to hold so many. The fog held tight to what they spoke. Then Betty McGuire sucked in her breath, looking past Judy Hendrick's face. Veeny Anderson touched her fingertips to the flesh above her heart and said, "I do declare, she is coming after all."

Malathy Joan emerged from the fog. Her hair and clothing cascaded down her like tendrils of shadow. Many shivered to see at last what had been a whisper and a longing. She held up her long skirts with slender fingers as she mounted the church steps. There was heaviness upon her, as though she were an old-time woman who stepped from a daguerreotype on a hallway wall and bore the years with her as she came. Her eyes looked out from dark and silent lands they did not know.

"Morning, folks," called Clement Foster. "This here's my new neighbor, everyone, this is Miss Malathy Joan."

Malathy Joan was not a beautiful woman, but as Veeny Anderson said later to Judy Hendrick, she was the kind to draw a man's eyes, with all that dark hair falling to her waist and her lithe way of moving, like a tree bending in a storm, and her big, black eyes.

"Hello," said Malathy in her scaly voice.

Paul Dingus hitched at the waist of his trousers. Jack Hendrick stood in the churchyard beside the front steps with his hands on the iron railing. Looking at her was like looking at branches in the snow, he thought, or feeling and smelling the ruffle of wind before a storm, when he would glance through the open door and then turn once again to the ledger, letting the bells sound the door shut.

"That's one plain, peculiar woman," mumbled Chad Mullins from beside him.

Noah Carpenter squared his shoulders and tugged at the cuffs of his black coat. Sunday clothes never fit him quite right. He must make his answer to her on that morning shrouded in God's mystery. Looking at Malathy Joan, he meant to make it as fine a thing as she deserved to have. His dream had given him pause, but now he reckoned he knew one thing. He might as well deny he stood there just because a little mist came down from the mountains as to deny her anything. She was a woman to do things for.

He stepped forward and held out his hand to welcome her. "Morning, Miss Malathy."

Gold flickered in the woman's dark eyes, and her thin lips curled up at the corners. "Hello, Noah," she said. She stretched out her hand and clasped his firmly.

Emmy watched them. In her frilled pink dress, she huddled close to her father and hoped she would not be addressed by Noah's kind, slow words.

"I was thinking I might ought to come up and have a look over that house," said Noah. He let go of Malathy's fingers. He had no hat brim to clutch, so he slipped both hands into his pockets. "And I was thinking you might ought to come, too, so you can tell me how you see it."

Veeny clasped her Bible and felt her breath bump against it. She did not know what to think. She had known Noah ever since his mother, Abilene, had carried him into town and left him with the boy's grandparents for good and all. He had been a mannered child and no trouble to anyone, and Noah had grown to be a man who knew what it was to humble himself before the Lord. Still, he was not friendly, to Veeny's way of thinking. He unbent himself for no one. She did not know what was happening now. She felt the damp seep in her throat. She would pray, she decided. She would put her old body down by her bed each night and ask God for Noah's soul and safety. She would plead that the Lord might send the stranger woman far, far down the road once more.

But Clement walked up as Noah spoke. "Well, now, why don't you come on up for dinner after service? This fog'll surely lift, and then you can head up and take a look at the place."

Noah nodded to Clement, to Malathy Joan. "Thank you, I reckon I'll do that."

Malathy Joan nodded in return. "Thank you for your help, Noah." She stood like the fragile pattern of tree limbs against a midnight sky.

Not many souls who had gathered in the churchyard that morning offered themselves up in worship. Men and women stood with open hymnals and sang with their backs stiffened and eyes lifted to nowhere. Most everybody only wished to turn about and see how Malathy Joan moved. In her long, black dress, she came into their consciousnesses as a silhouette in a dim, twilight room, as a darkness that sat beside them now and then in the long winter and hurt their hearts with remembering. They pressed the hand of son or husband as the preacher spoke on Proverbs and the strange woman in those pages whose house and paths inclined unto the dead. The preacher reminded the congregation of the destruction brought about by the Lord, of its awesome power and terrible finality.

But Noah Carpenter figured differently. From his seat in the bare, wooden pew, he looked across the aisle at Malathy Joan once during the service. People were bowing their heads to pray, and he watched her close her eyes. Her lashes lay as dark fringes against her skin. Her face was empty and waiting. He knew that if folks in Beulah Creek could not see that there was blessing in everything that woman did, then they would never see blessing on the earth, because they did not know what it looked like.

The mist had burned away by the time the service ended, and the land was burnished with the last gold of summer. People left the churchhouse in clumps of color, their coats draped over their arms. All about them, the mountains folded strength and beauty like a glorious fortress, and above them shone a gentle blue. Clement and Emmy and Malathy Joan crossed Beulah Creek together and climbed to the Fosters' house to make ready for the rest of the day. Noah Carpenter joined them afterwards, in his work clothes once more, and they sat down to a dinner of country ham biscuits, green beans, and canned pears.

After the meal, Clement took up the Sunday paper from the coffee table. He allowed he would sit on the front porch awhile and enjoy the sun and the air and the sound of the chimes. The thought of the climb up to the old house wore him out. So Malathy Joan put the dishes into the washer, then she and Noah and Emmy went out the door and higher up the hill beneath the bright and blessed autumn sun.

They thrust the grass from before them as they went through the afternoon, and the feathery heads nodded at their passage. Tiny winged things buzzed all about them, bursting now and then into sudden gleams that darted among the stalks. Noah raised his arm to his forehead and looked out across the creek bottom. It was a sight to him, the way the mountains were put together. He did not know how rock and soil and tree could be so soft-seeming, crumpled all over like fabric. "You can see a far piece, up here," he said.

Malathy Joan nodded. Her fingers strayed to the silver pendant that beat against her chest. "I do hope so. I hope to see peace when I walk out of my door, and when I walk in again." The grinning windows began to peer at them. She breathed a sad sound. "I wonder what Jess saw, from up here." Her eyes were hollows into the dark where no light came.

Noah followed Malathy's gaze up the hill. The air felt heavier, as though they had got into a dark patch of forest where the branches hung low and leafy over their heads. But the land was clear. They walked on. Malathy Joan's long hair was blowing, her dress moving like dark things in sleep.

"Reckon Jess'll come out to you, when you're living there?" asked Emmy.

"Perhaps," the woman said. "The house did not feel empty to me."

Noah scratched the back of his head before he answered. "Not many places around here are what you'd call empty."

"No," said Malathy Joan, "that's true. I haven't forgotten what that's like. I grew up near the mountains."

"Whereabouts?" he asked her.

"Edenston. My parents taught at the college there."

Noah knew the town, thirty miles or so from Millsborough, down in the lowlands, nestled in the hills.

"My mama was a Greenberry," Emmy said. She ran up and took hold of Malathy Joan's hand with both of hers. "But they've all gone away now. They've gone to see Jesus, or they've all gone away." Clutching that hand was for Emmy like speaking sacred words, hallowed be thy name. She had watched Malathy's hands over the past days and marveled at the grace with which they moved. And now they had come to reclaim the desolation, a calling she could not imagine for herself. She would love this woman forever.

They approached the house. "The weatherboarding seems all right," said Noah. He set to rolling up his sleeves. He walked no more slowly nor softly than he would walk anywhere else. "Hold just a minute, and let me see this," he said.

He stepped onto the flat stone step. Then his boots made solid thudding sounds upon the front porch. The wood cried out like a strange bird but seemed sturdy enough. He recalled his dream of the other night.

"There's liable to be loose boards in here," he said, nearing the doorway. "You might want to stay outside, Emmy."

"No," said Emmy. She would not let go of the stranger woman's hand. "Don't make me stay without you, Malathy Joan." Emmy had never been this close to the house before. She looked up at the greenery that grew across the window. The whispers rose to her like vapor, like steam from a boiling pot. She could not tell their name. A ringing came to her ears, and she felt her blood move. It was worse than she had thought, far worse.

"You'll be with us, Emmy." Malathy walked onto the porch, leading the soft child. She looked carefully for the broken boards, the water damage, the rot of years, but did not see it. "What do you see, Noah?" she asked.

He stepped over the threshold, and then he was in the house. He did not know what he expected. He stood in a room with a stone hearth and an overturned wooden table at the front of it. The leavings of a rag rug lay on the floor.

"Don't know as I can tell yet," he said.

He heard Emmy and Malathy Joan follow him in. A sweet, dusty smell seemed almost to drift away as they entered. Emmy sneezed.

"Bless you," said Malathy.

From the front to the back of the house ran a wall, and in it was a firmly closed door. At the back of the house was an ancient cook stove with other kitchen furnishings and another door, likewise shut, which looked to lead outside towards Sumac Hill. A rocking chair stood before the back window.

"So that was what she saw," said Malathy Joan. She walked across the room with Emmy to the rocking chair and sat down. She turned her face to the curtain of ivy. "She must have been waiting for someone. I wonder how long."

Noah peered up at the rafters. "There's plenty of wondering to do here."

Emmy squatted beside the rocking chair and reached for Malathy Joan. Jess Greenberry must have waited there for the calling, Emmy decided, the opening within of soft magenta. She felt her fingers tingle and a quiver along the back of her neck. "Smells like lilacs in here," she whispered.

"I smell forgotten things," said Malathy. "Forsaken things."

Noah thought of a woman made out of cold fog, seated with Malathy Joan at supper. He was not sure whether to mind such a thing or not.

All at once, Emmy heard the house reaching for them. The whispers were thorns and tendrils of a terrible plant that grew forever. They spoke her name until there was no meaning left. She wanted to shrink down inside herself until she disappeared.

"I say Jesus," she murmured and felt the house move off her some. "Our words don't go nowhere in here."

Malathy pressed her hand. "It's just that she listens hard, maybe."

Noah swallowed. He did not much care to have Mrs. Greenberry's dead ears taking in their talk. "I'm going to go have a look at the rest of the house."

Malathy nodded. "I'll sit here a moment, please."

"You reckon there's snakes in here?" said Emmy suddenly, lifting her face to the dark woman.

"They won't hurt you if you leave them alone," said Noah. He walked to the closed door in the middle of the house. "Just watch you don't step on one."

Emmy shuddered. The door groaned, and Noah's steps took him from their sight. She was glad of being right where she was. "You must be very good to come here," she said to Malathy Joan.

"If goodness brought me, it wasn't my own," said Malathy.

Emmy did not understand the ache that rose, throbbing through her in bursts, until she wanted suddenly something to love. She curled her palm about the leg of the chair and stroked it down to the rocker, feeling how very dry the wood was. She did not see how the dark woman could keep fear lashed within her silver pendant and not feel it near. But then there was none she knew so holy as Malathy Joan, who knew what it was to die and to rise.

In the other room, Noah clutched the bedpost, feeling the smooth curve of the wood. The bed sagged from the weight of all those years. He could smell the musty cornhusk mattress beneath the crumpled blankets. He listened to Malathy Joan's voice from the other room. He reckoned she belonged there as much as any of them, weary and stark as she was, like a creekbed in winter, like a huddle of stones in November rain. He let go the bedpost and wiped his palms on his jeans legs. He would be the last one to deny her. He knew this house should be tumbling down all over, but his hard, black eyes saw evidence of sound wood. To what purpose, he did not know. But if she believed, that was enough for him.

That night in the crisp dark, the windowpanes of the town opened gold on the black ground, as television screens glowed upon bodies and deep couches. Everyone in Beulah Creek knew that strange doings were among them every day. Trees drank stories of the land from below the soil. The rocks of mountains knew happenings that only God knew else. So heads only nodded as lips whispered that Emmy Foster had seen a rattlesnake in the old Greenberry house, and Noah Carpenter had killed it by crushing its head with the heel of his boot. It was a terrible omen and chilled more folks right to the bone than any wind of fall. Not everyone in the town gave credence to such a tale. But those who heard and did believe it were coming to understand Malathy Joan as one who stirred from darkest corners the wraiths of their sleep and the hates of their hearts. Those people began to feel their hearts go skittering at the mention of her name.

Though Grandma Barnes never heeded such idleness as what was being told of the carpenter, she had her own misgivings. Standing on the front porch with the dog, she smelled the bitterness and the withering in the air. The year was going. She looked at Sumac Hill high above the Greenberry house, high above the town, and knew dead bones anchored the roots of the trees and mountains. She hissed and shook her head. The stranger woman could not go and air out rooms and hang up fresh curtains like Jess Greenberry was gone from Beulah Creek. There was one thing everlasting in this world, and that was the crumpled toothless grin that blackened the leaves on the trees and snatched people's breath from their mouths. Beulah Creek huddled always in its shadow, and Jess Greenberry's house was its dwellingplace, and long after all the cursed business of mankind swept the puny little town off the earth, Sumac Hill with its graveyard would keep standing, because time's waters didn't run so high. That was what she knew, what she had always known, and the knowledge gave her power, the secret power of knowing, as Lucien Brown had once named it, as he had taught her.

Grandma Barnes gripped the head of her cane. She had seen that young man's face too many times in Beulah Creek and had come to know at last the power that removed it.

Once as a child eleven years old, Hazel Barnes was wandering along the creek towards dawn. Sometimes she crept out as her mother slept, and other times, her mother was called away to some townswoman's side to help with a birth. That night, her mother had slept, and Hazel was headed upstream and into the woods on the slopes below the Greenberry house, scant days before its builder would leave it forever, but long, long before the trees were cut and Clement Foster's new home raised on the Greenberry land.

Hazel had been a shadow in the trees as the sun came up, and as she crouched behind the trunk of an oak to relieve herself, she heard a shout above her and the scuffling of leaves. She saw two men up the slope, struggling together. Except for the leaves and the night sounds of the woods, there was no noise. Sometimes one of them raised his voice, but that was all.

She kept still and watched, afraid a little, until finally one of the men threw the other to the ground and beat him with something until he stopped moving. Nothing else moved. She stayed behind the tree while the dead man was covered with leaves. Then the living one wiped his brow and turned and walked back through the trees toward his house. That was how she witnessed Saul Greenberry kill Lucien Brown. To the rest of Beulah Creek, Lucien, a stranger man, disappeared that day from the town and afterwards from all memory save hers.

She had never spoken Lucien's name again after what she had done, sure not after Jess Greenberry was cut down from the rafters, the darkest, most awful part of that whole wretched affair to Grandma Barnes. She figured she would see again what had been before, hatred beaten against the bones of a living man and still worse, now the stranger woman had come among them with her desire to stir the house once more to life.

But the troubles of the people of Beulah Creek on that night, and her part in them, Malathy Joan did not know. She merely lay in the brass bed in the darkness of the Fosters' spare bedroom and looked above her. Her arm was folded behind her head. She breathed the intimate air and held her life full in her lungs. The Greenberry house waited for her up the hill. She knew dark and terrible things had happened within its walls. She knew, also, that dark and terrible things had happened within her. And she was living still.

Her chest tightened and then opened wider than she could remember. She believed, in the end, the house she had chosen could be hers at last, if she lived well enough, if she loved well enough. She would pay for it with everything she had sold, and yet there would be safety enough to live on for years to come.

IV

The early October days turned brisk and smelled of golden grass. Most Beulah Creek dwellers were moved, feeling the pull of some slight sadness, but glad of the sunlight on the colored hills. Betty McGuire baked a batch of ginger cookies. Veeny Anderson sliced the very reddest tomato to make tomato sandwiches, taking two of them over to old Anson Bledsoe who was badly crippled since he had fallen some months ago. And at dusk, Judy Hendrick thought it a pity to have to shut the windows against the spiced smell of woodsmoke, but she felt the cold drawing down around her, and besides, she had always been more than a bit uneasy about what might be creeping out there in the dark.

In the winsome, sweet-smelling mornings, Malathy Joan lifted her head to the sky and looked far, far out across the land. She could not see what would come. She saw only the work of her hands as she labored beside Noah Carpenter. She felt the good wood and the ache in her back and the blisters rubbed by the hammer. She tasted the sandwiches and the lemonade she prepared for the noonday dinners they shared, sitting out in the sunlight and the soft, quiet wind. She listened to Noah's breathing and was glad of someone to share her meals.

After dinner, she walked in the dark rooms and looked for Jess Greenberry, thinking over the words she might say to the wandering spirit. As she looked at the ancient furniture and filthy rugs, she remembered things she had never known, like the color of the tablecloth and the pattern of the china. Her body tingled with her heartbeat, a feeling that was neither fear nor happiness. It simply was, and she sought to understand her place in it. These were days of laying up treasure. She held them dear, fingering them gently as she fingered the silver pendant she wore.

One day, Malathy Joan sat after dinner in the grass in her brown sleeveless blouse and cargo pants. She looked down to the town in the creek bottom, to the white church spire and Grandma Barnes's house and the glittering beaded water that wended its way past. It would be a comfortable thing, to be neighbor to it all. She would not have to sit in that rocking chair as Jess Greenberry might have done, waiting for it to pass her window. There was work given her to do. Her fingers grazed the lovely bloom of a fire pink in the short grass. There were dozens of the spring wildflowers growing there now, all about their dinner place.

Noah was sitting nearby, a little behind her, in his well-worn overalls that he kept so very clean. As she touched the flower, he said, "I think you ought to know. A lot of folks are thinking it's an unnatural thing you're doing, moving here to Beulah Creek and fixing on Mrs. Greenberry's house to live in."

"Yes," she said.

She rather liked Noah Carpenter. He was a strange man. He removed his hat in the presence of women in the town but didn't seem very inclined to marry any of them. The people of Beulah Creek, and Veeny Anderson especially, wished that he would talk more and say much less. When he walked past the small gathering of men in front of Jack Hendrick's store and greeted them with a nod and a word or two, he walked alone and left alone. If she were neighbor to all of Beulah Creek, Malathy Joan decided she would keep Noah for her friend.

She turned to look at him. "And you, what are you thinking?"

His hand gripped a tuft of grass. He leaned his head to one side before answering. "Those flowers there don't usually show their heads until spring. And folks don't usually come to Beulah Creek looking to stay. But I know one thing, it's not the sort of place you can leave easy. Not everybody has taken the trouble to find that out." His voice came with a painstaking care that put a kind of tenderness in his words.

"Where did you go, when you left?" she asked.

He did not seem troubled by the question. Still, they were quiet together for several minutes before he spoke.

"Out by the sea," he said and looked off at the scarlet treetops across the narrow valley. "I figured there'd be plenty of room out there. Not so many people banging away at everything. And it is something else, what-all you can see when you look out across that water. There's storms that come up out there, too, like nothing you'd ever see. It puts you in mind of God."

Her eyes grew darker. "And still you came back."

Noah shrugged. "There's such a thing as seeing too far, I reckon. I don't know. I figured it was time to come home."

He was silent, and they watched the birds flying away to other lands. The sky was the passionate blue of farewell.

"The mountains can take a hold of you," he said, "and those are stone chains fastened way down at the roots of things."

Malathy Joan nodded. "I will take the chains that I find here. I lived in the city for many years," she said, simply, her voice scraped bare of hatred and grief. Her hand clasped the silver circle and traced the pattern of the cross within.

Noah watched the movement of her fingers. "I hear tell the city can be a lonesome place."

"I don't mind lonesome," she said. "I don't mind it the way some people do." To her, it had its own loveliness, like a warm spot on the floor where the evening sun came to visit. "But that wasn't what came to me there."

She would have told him, if he had asked her. She was not ashamed of what had come to her, of the careless life she had made, though it had given great hurt, even terrible damage, to others. It had taken all the joy from her eyes and made her heart a brittle thing, and there were those who would draw back from her, their faces full of redness and fumbling, of pity, or even of blame, at the words she might say.

But he did not ask. The long, stern gash of his mouth said only, "Around here, a body's got to make their own kind of room. Though I don't reckon that'll be any too hard for you."

She knew then that Noah Carpenter spoke to her both in warning and in kindness, that he believed her without fear. Her lips gave their pale smile.

"I was driving," she said, "I was driving away from the horizon. And when I came onto the road to Beulah Creek, I found the morning on the mountaintops, and it all came back to me. I could be here." She looked at him, and there was gold in her eyes as she remembered. "So I am here."

And Noah, looking at her, was not at all sorry for that. "It took some real doing to leave everything you owned," he said. "To come away with no more than you brought with you."

"I have all I need," she said. "I sold everything I had to be here. Except for this." Her fingers touched the pendant he had never seen her lack. "It was given me by a truly good woman. For remembrance, to keep myself together. I needed it then. I need it still."

Noah moved his head. "Somebody's done a good thing for you, then," he said.

"Yes, I have my life because of it. Many have given me kindness, and I am thankful every day," she said. "Every day."

Her eyes looked so warm to him always, like the hope of hearthside after long hours of toil. She was a right handsome woman, the more Noah thought about it, with her well-made bones and her antique eyes and her face like a fine, dark wooden door.

He brushed the breadcrumbs from the faded denim of his overalls and watched the ants scramble about in the grass among the fire pinks. They were good creatures, hard-working and faithful. To them, the shower of bread was manna from heaven, strange and inexplicable, and that was how it was with a lot of things. Folks just had to be willing to receive without asking a lot of questions. Noah rubbed the back of his neck near his shoulder, where the work knotted him up sometimes. All he knew was, his own dreams weren't too troublesome those days, and the Greenberry house didn't look so wild anymore, with the grass cut back so he could bring up the van in the mornings. Malathy Joan set her hands to strong, strange workings, but whatever else she had come to do among them, she had at least come to build and not to destroy. He favored building himself.

In the afternoons, when Noah Carpenter and Malathy Joan would be hard at work, building, Emmy Foster climbed the hill to the Greenberry house after school, treading the path Noah had mowed, to sit among the fire pinks and read her Bible. She was not so afraid to sit there in the late afternoon sunshine and listen to hammers pounding resurrection into the old boards. She gnawed strands of hair, intent, as the pages of King James English gave her words for the things she knew, like glory and righteousness and the gracious giving word, unto.

Sometimes she ate her favorite cheese crackers while she read, and sometimes she drank a grape soda she had bought from Jack Hendrick's store. Always, she was glad of her life and the new things that Malathy Joan wrought among them.

Emmy hungered for a shining new Greenberry house that burgeoned with lilac blossoms and the Mary Magdalene in a long white dress hanging the bedsheets out to dry. In the garden would be a world full of light, wondrous and strange as the throbbing of her heart, and Emmy would open herself to it, the most perfect calling, like the sunshine when it slipped down inside her. In those days, Emmy said a Bible verse over and over beneath her breath, no matter where she might be, "They shall build the old wastes, they shall raise up the former desolations."

But not all the thoughts in Beulah Creek were as pleasant as hers. After one of Emmy Foster's trips to the store for grape soda, accompanied by her innocent remarks, Judy Hendrick learned that the ground about the Greenberry house grew patches of spring flowers. Judy told Veeny Anderson over the telephone, and Veeny told Betty McGuire and anyone else she could think of. And there were many more tales to tell of Malathy Joan. Strange crews of men from Millsborough and other lowland places came and worked on the house with her and Noah. There was a refrigerator that used no electricity and an expensive cookstove. People whispered about her money, where it could come from, how she could spend and never do a day's work. Some believed she came from a wealthy family, while some thought she had once married well or had made a pretty sum in business before coming to Beulah Creek. Some arched their eyebrows significantly and allowed that perhaps it was not day's work she did. Wives and mothers began to keep careful eyes on their sons and husbands.

Jack Hendrick was starting to be uneasy. He hadn't really given the stranger woman much thought, he told himself, but now he noticed how his heart jumped whenever the bells rang in the store. He was not sure what he would do if she came with her eyes like moonlight and asked in her brittle voice for something he didn't have.

One evening he told Judy that he reckoned he would go outside and look at the sunset a while, since he had been cooped up in the store all day. Judy looked at him sharply and told him it was getting dark mighty quick, and he answered her and said that was how it happened when the sun went down, and then he was out the front door before Judy could say anything else.

And so he ended up, as he had intended, at the house of Noah Carpenter. He headed first to Noah's back door but saw the light on in the workshop, so he crossed the bare strip of earth where straggling tufts of grass poked up through the dark red clay. The door was open, and Noah stood at the worktable with his back towards the door. Jack could not see what Noah was doing, except that his shoulders and arms were moving, and that he seemed intent on his work.

Jack took care to make a little noise as he walked up to the door. He scuffed his shoes against the hard-packed earth and cleared his throat. "Howdy there," he called. "It sure is a nice evening out here, ain't it?"

Noah did not turn his head for a moment. Then he looked over his shoulder. "Evening, Jack." He gave a solemn nod. "You and Judy doing all right these days?"

"I reckon," said Jack. "We're making do, anyhow."

Noah turned around, tugging a piece of cloth out of his hip pocket and wiping his hands. "Well, you come to see me about something. You-all still thinking about kitchen cabinets in the spring?"

Jack had not thought about cabinets for a good while. He thought about them now, scratching the back of his neck. "We hadn't talked about it lately, but I reckon she's pretty well set on the idea." But even as he said this, a dark, doubting feeling crept its way along the pit of his stomach. So he said straight away, "Fact is, though, I didn't come to see you on account of the cabinets."

Noah put the cloth back into his hip pocket. He said nothing, and neither did Jack, who felt the darkness damp and heavy in his stomach like a fog in a creek bottom. He started to open his mouth, but then Noah nodded and said, "All right." So Noah stood there, and Jack could not tell what the man was thinking, because Noah always spoke quiet and slow and humble, but his face was another thing altogether, not exactly inviting company.

"Well," said Jack, dragging the word out, and then he felt foolish. The whole thing felt foolish. So he started talking. "You know I don't put much store in what folks say. Judy comes home talking such fool things I can scarce stay in the room to hear, let alone tell them over." As he spoke, Jack kept close watch on Noah's face, looking for some change, perhaps a sharpening behind the eyes. "But you know that she . . . she ain't like anyone I've ever laid eyes on." He didn't have to say who she was. Anyone in Beulah Creek would know. He thought he did just as well not to say her name for the spell it had over all in the town. "And I don't know what to make of it. I don't."

Noah's face did not move as he listened to Jack. He stayed silent for several minutes. Then he tilted his head a little and said, "Might be there's no need to go on so. She's howsoever she is, never mind what any of us cares to do about it."

"I reckon that's a fact," said Jack. A simple emptiness entered his stomach now, and he could say what he wanted. "You've got the house about ready?"

Noah looked at him with eyes that were hard and flat, and his face was grim. But he spoke with careful kindness. "She's going up there in two, three weeks, likely, and says she means to have a few folks to supper soon after. She wouldn't mind you coming, if you wanted. I could ask her for you."

Jack stared. His mouth filled with cold earth.

"You and Judy both," said Noah. "She'd like that."

Jack did not dare to shake his head, or God would strike him where he stood. "You know Judy wouldn't set foot up there. And she'd never let me back in the house again if I went. That's the Lord's truth." Jack could not imagine what would happen if ever that woman with her doe eyes looked across a table at him, if ever her brown hand waited on the other side of the bread basket. He didn't want to imagine it. He would jump for the rest of his life at the ringing of the bells in his store.

"Thank you anyhow," he said, and indeed, he was very thankful to be saying so before Noah offered any such thing to him again. "Reckon I'd better head on, or Judy'll lock up with me still outside." He backed away.

Noah said only, "Let me know when you-all decide on those cabinets."

"Sure," said Jack. And then, to be interested, he added, "Looks like you're working away at something there." He couldn't see what it was, because Noah stood and blocked it from his view.

"That's so," said Noah, "but it's near about done now." Even as he spoke, he turned back to the worktable. "You have a good evening, Jack."

There was nothing more to do but leave.

"Good night," Jack said and walked off. He walked quickly. It was quite cold now, and the night sky seemed much too dark and empty, with only here and there a tiny star like a silver bell to clink on the wind. He noticed their small, shivering beauty scattered above the silent hills. He sighed. But he wanted very much to see his front door, and even better, the kitchen light burning through the window. He folded his arms to keep warm as he walked.

Noah lingered in the cold awhile longer, working. His hands moved, and the light in the workshop was bright enough, and although he noticed the cold, he noticed the tiny dovetails even more and labored so that they would fit smoothly together.

When at last he finished his work and took it with him into the house, he was no longer troubled. It was Jack that had troubled him, he decided as he headed down the hall, it was all that wandering around that never came to what a body set out for and only meant faithlessness in the end. Not that he had no faith in Jack, for Jack was a good man, but Jack had little faith in the way of things, in her way of things. And so Jack was out admiring the sunset and walking up and down the road and didn't understand any of it at all.

Beside his lamp and his Bible, Noah put the little wooden box on the table next to his bed. It was good work, he decided, looking at it, running his finger over the surfaces, and it satisfied him. He didn't rightly know what to call it, this thing he had made to keep the one treasure she had, but he wasn't about to let that trouble him. He would put it into her hands all the same.

Later, as he was washing his face, he thought about the faces he would see at the supper in a few weeks' time, and about her face most of all. Malathy Joan would watch the evening pass with her eyes like dark rivers, the gold flickering in them when the waters moved. Hers was a face that he could talk to or be quiet with, and she seemed always to understand. And later, after he had turned out the lamp and rested his head on the pillow, he thought something else, that all those whining songs on the radio weren't worth a damn. He went to sleep, then, seeing her face like dusk on the mountains in dreams of distant home.

All around Beulah Creek, the people turned again from their windows, wishing for magic, for benevolence, and closed their doors, shutting themselves away to await the dying time. It would not be long in coming. The first frost would visit them one night very soon.

V

The last gold and crimson leaves dropped down through cold sunlight on the day Malathy Joan knocked on Grandma Barnes's front door. The grass had already ceased to grow, and the crumpled brown husks of zinnias still lingered in a few front yards.

With that way she had of moving her angular body, darkness upon darkness rippling down those long bones, the woman raised her hand and rapped her knuckles against the door. Inside the house, the dog barked with vehemence. Then the door came open, and there was Hazel Barnes, bowed and weathered, but looking right up at the stranger woman with keen, cutting eyes. Those old eyes had looked at all kinds of things in the wild, berries and roots and mushrooms. Those eyes could tell the difference between wholesome and poison. With a kind of fragile hesitance, Malathy Joan stood two steps back from the door, her hands clasped at her waist, her eyes luminous. The dog kept barking, so that the air shuddered with shrill bursts of noise.

Grandma Barnes turned her head over her shoulder and hissed. The dog fell silent.

"What did you come for?" said Grandma Barnes, turning back at once. She squinted up into the dark face. "Is it done?"

"Yes," said Malathy Joan. Hers was a face that had looked once into winter woods and was chilled forever. It had grown lean and hollow from the cold. "I am going there tomorrow."

Grandma Barnes grunted. "And then what'll you do?"

"I suppose I'll see." Malathy Joan raised her right thumb and forefinger and touched the silver pendant.

"I reckon you see enough," said Grandma Barnes.

Malathy Joan gave her weary smile. "Not yet."

Grandma Barnes stepped forward. "What did you come for?" Her gnarled hand gripped the cane firmly. "It ain't likely you come to pass the time of day." She had known right off that this woman was bent on dipping her long-handled spoon into the swirl and foam that was Beulah Creek and stirring no matter what might arise.

"I'm having supper Thursday night," said Malathy Joan, slowly, "and I've come to ask you to join us."

There was no sound in the world but the cold rattle of leaves against the ground.

"No," said Grandma Barnes. And she shook her head. "No."

"You could tell what more you know of Jess Greenberry so I will understand," said Malathy Joan. Her face seemed to slip in and out of shadows. "I should like to understand. You could look over the house, so you will know that I mean to look after things there."

The words brushed into Grandma Barnes like a brown moth flying against a human face in the dark. When Hazel had last gone to that house, she had rapped on the door and told the beautiful, false-hearted woman inside, out of sorrow, out of horror, out of some dark vengeance, what murder she had witnessed the day before, on the slopes below among the trees. This time, she meant to keep well clear of this woman's affairs.

"I done told you, no." Grandma Barnes turned her back to Malathy Joan. "Maybe you can see a far piece, but you sure don't hear too well. Now get on off my porch and on your way."

And the door banged shut. Some minutes still, Malathy Joan lingered there, her face more sorrowful than before, perhaps, and then turned and headed back through the town.

When the sun went down the next night, there wasn't a soul in Beulah Creek who hadn't heard from Veeny Anderson, who lived near, what had happened, how the stranger woman had tried to lure Grandma Barnes up to the old Greenberry place. And even the following day, most folks were still taking and then giving the story again as a solemn warning to all.

But a few held their tongue, and Grandma Barnes herself was one, finding it futile to speak a thing to death, watching a fly scuttle across her windowpane. As the Preacher said in the Bible, if one paid heed to such, maybe the past was what was yet to come. But then to reveal or to stay quiet, to act or refrain, it all was fraught alike. Any way she turned might hasten and not impede what would come. The past had a life of its own.

She unlocked the back door and cracked it, even as the fly on her window hummed on its jerky, muddled path. She watched the insect hesitate. Then she snatched him with her cupped hand and tossed him out the door. He would die out there, she knew and had grown weary with knowing, but she was not about to swat him. Grandma Barnes pressed the door shut again, and the cold dwindled about her ankles.

Elsewhere in Beulah Creek, Noah Carpenter had just as little use for all the talk of Malathy Joan, but he had his own reasons. That evening, he went walking as the sun went down. He walked up the road and over the little bridge that spanned the creek and then up the hill towards the Fosters' house. Carrying the wooden box he had made, he walked without hurry but with steadiness all the same. All along the creek bottom he saw little, yellow lights where folks lived. But up the mountain slopes, the forests were empty and waiting for the night to come down to them. It put him in mind of Malathy Joan's face with her eyes closed in church. Where Noah walked, there shone only the light from the Fosters', and, farther up the hill and smaller, the light that was the Greenberry house. Noah had seen it last night as he slept. For much of the night, he had carried the wooden box in a dream through tall grass towards that light.

Clement and Emmy Foster were just coming out onto their front porch as Noah walked by. It wasn't so dark yet but Noah could tell that Clement was in Sunday clothes, and Emmy had a ribbon in her hair.

Clement lifted a hand. "Hold up, there, stranger, and we'll all go together, if that don't bother you none."

Noah stopped and put his right hand into his coat pocket. The weather radio had promised a cold night. "Evening, Clement, Miss Emmy."

Emmy was clinging to her father's arm. She looked down where she put her feet. "Evening, Noah," she said, softly.

The windchimes rang a little when the wind stirred, making the night sound even colder. Clement shivered as he and his daughter walked over to where Noah stood. "Let's hope you hung them boards right, or we'll all be stiff as boards, sitting up there in that drafty old place." Clement chuckled, though his insides chilled at the thought of the wind whistling through cracks and making strange, hollow sounds in the house.

"It'll be warm enough, I reckon," said Noah. He knew how very sound that house had seemed before he ever took a hammer to it.

So Noah and the Fosters walked on together. It seemed to Noah a good place to be, headed up that way, so near the quiet and the sky and the trees lifted up in glory as the sun sank into darkness. He kept the little box close to him.

When they came to the Greenberry house, the trees had gone into the dark of the mountains. It wasn't nearly as cold up there. Emmy heard the whispering grass and saw the rocking chair through the front window now. The whispers passed through her as she saw the chair waiting there, and she felt herself so vacant and dark and horrible that nothing could ever fill her. She could not even cry out. But then, through the storm door, she could see Malathy Joan coming from the kitchen. The woman was coming from the rich, honey light and stood then in the doorway, her hand opening the storm door. Emmy let go her father's arm and rushed onto the porch. She could breathe again, she could open her mouth now, and she said, "Welcome home, I missed you."

Malathy Joan stretched out her arms and clasped the child against her. Over the girl's head, she spoke to the two men. "Hello. Please come in." She guided Emmy into the house, her arm about the girl's shoulders, then held the storm door open as Clement and Noah came up the steps. Noah took off his hat.

"Evening, Miss Malathy," said Clement, nodding to her. "It sure was nice of you to have us to supper."

"I'm pleased you've come," she said. She had braided her hair into a single plait, and she wore a dress of deep, heavy purple. She was barefoot, and the silver pendant glowed there against her chest.

Clement followed his daughter into the Greenberry house, and then Noah came to the door.

"Hello, Noah," said Malathy Joan. She stretched out her hand as she did most Sunday mornings when they met down in Beulah Creek.

Noah clutched both his hat and the wooden box. So he said, "I've brought you something."

"Yes," she said, and smiled. "You have, and always do."

Then Noah held the box toward her, and her smile receded into the shadows. "Thank you," she said, more quietly, taking the box. They both came into the front room. She looked at the lovely thing she held, touching it with her long fingers. "You made this."

"I meant it for a housewarming present," said Noah. He clutched his hat with both hands until his neck and shoulders ached. "For your necklace."

She lifted her head then, and her eyes were bright with gold. "That was very good of you." She knew that about him, that he made things true and good, had known it for the time she lived in Beulah Creek. She reached her fingers and briefly touched the skin of his hand.

Noah did not say anything.

"What is it?" said Emmy, getting up from the couch. Malathy Joan turned toward the girl and held the box for Emmy to see. Emmy breathed, "Oh, it's so pretty!" Clement was looking about the room and saying, "You sure have fixed up this old place." All the while, Noah noticed the bend of the woman's slender fingers about the box. He studied her face. What he saw there satisfied him. Her eyes were truer than anything he had ever known, though he could not rightly say that he understood what she looked to find. He only knew, as he had believed, that she welcomed gifts as she gave the ones she possessed, with a solemn grace.

Clement had no need to worry about the cold that night, for no one who spent that evening at the Greenberry house had ever been more pleasantly warm and full. Every room seemed to glow with firelight, and the air smelled faintly and drowsily of lilacs. The supper was herbed chicken, mashed potatoes, peas, and red cabbage and apples, with great slices of crusty, buttered bread. Like all the food that Malathy Joan prepared, it tasted in new and miraculous dimensions, down to the store-bought salt that somehow acquired flavor and meaning when added to her meal. Malathy asked Noah to say grace, and though

Clement had rarely heard his friend pray aloud, he thought it a fine blessing, if a little short, all about hands and work and simple joys. Listening to Noah's words, Clement figured if any ghosts were lurking about, they couldn't do any harm on a night like this, when there was nothing but good, wholesome words in the hearts of friends and good, wholesome food being passed from hand to hand.

After supper, they left the kitchen, walled away now from the front of the house with a doorway for passage. They sat in the front room with the new little wooden box on the mantel and the old rocking chair in front of the window. Emmy drifted off to sleep first, listening to her father talking, and then, during a pause in the conversation, Clement fell asleep as well. The pause softened into the peace that comes with a late hour and a low-burning fire and a quiet that is not ashamed of itself.

Malathy Joan sat in the rocking chair and looked at the mantelpiece, as though she saw there the days she hoped for, and the evenings longed for, and pondered what they might bring after all. Noah looked mostly at the fire.

It was nearly half an hour before Malathy said, in her low, crackling voice. "It was good of you to help me, Noah. It was good of you to come."

Noah looked at the fire and tapped his hat against his knee. "I don't reckon it's particularly good of me," he said after awhile. It was the only honest thing he could think to say.

"You don't know what you've done." The firelight in her eyes only seemed to make them darker, as though there were holes, caverns, inside of her that the light could never reach. "I had almost stopped believing that there was life anywhere. I've been . . . gone . . . so long. But I believe this house has begun to answer me."

Noah swallowed against the cold place that was opening in his chest. It was like talking to someone in a dream, where the words meant too many things and he understood them all until he awoke the next morning. "What do you plan on answering back?"

"I'm going to plant a garden."

He looked hard at her. "It might be a little late for that."

"It's always been too late with me." She shook her head. "It's going to be the right time this time. The right place."

He didn't know what to say to that. There were things that were true enough, and then there was the winter. "A body's got to do what they believe is right," he said, finally.

She turned her head from the fireplace. The light and shadow shifted in her eyes and across her face. "You believe me." It was only half a question.

He looked at his hat where it rested on his knees. "There's a whole lot I don't know," he said. "And it don't bother me, that I don't know." He thought of Jack Hendrick wandering around half-blind in the sunset. No, Noah didn't believe exactly, but he could accept that things were the way they were.

She smiled. There was peace in her smile. "I think it will be a good winter, here among neighbors. You will all have to come back and share it with me."

Noah considered his hat thoughtfully. "Thank you. Reckon I'll do that." He raised his eyes, then, to watch the logs burn. The silence hissed from the fireplace, and he recalled what Grandma Barnes had said, that it would be a right cold winter this year. A body could do worse than seek out a warm hearth and good folks to sit nearby and talk about things or perhaps to let the quiet be heard in the flickering colors and shadows. In the stillness, he wasn't especially fearful of what he might hear.

And neither was Malathy Joan afraid, when her friends had gone back down the hill and left her in the Greenberry house with the faint smell of lilacs stirring in the dark. She listened as she dressed in her long cotton nightgown and washed her face. She listened as she unfastened the pendant and chain and placed them in their handmade box on the mantel. She was listening still as she knelt on the hardwood floor beside her bed. She sat upon her bony knees for some time, hearing only her breath and the murmur of her heart.

Though all of Beulah Creek later said otherwise, said that the kindred souls had called one another from the dark places of the world to behold each other first on the first night they lived together, the spirit of Jess Greenberry never walked in Malathy Joan's eyes, nor yet her heart, on that night nor on any night she had already spent there. When Malathy finally slipped her legs beneath the sheet and rested her head on her pillow, not a little regret eddied through her stomach. There can be peace here, she thought, and I would share it with you, poor woman, lost woman. I would know your suffering and your story, to make you whole. What everyone else in Beulah Creek trembled to believe, was what the stranger woman with her everlasting eyes most wanted to see.

VI

The snow came early to Beulah Creek that year. It sifted across the mountains like a fine sleeping powder. The people stumbled about the town, their minds heavy with wool and flannel, and they blinked at the name of the stranger woman. They struggled to know if the tales of her were anything more than heaps of brightly-colored, translucent candies. No one cared to climb the hill to see if the Greenberry house were truly wreathed in primroses in November. No one bothered to ask Noah Carpenter of the woman, for he would only shrug and trudge away in his boots and wool jacket through the snow. Until the times she herself appeared in the town, dark and shiveringly clear like a blackbird against the grey sky, most people in Beulah Creek wrinkled their foreheads to recall if she were really anything more than a blowing shape from a dream. They only wished to crawl among their couches and pillows and wrap themselves away beside their lemon and tangerine fires. There they would sleep as the night passed into twilight before returning again.

But up around the Greenberry house, there was no snow. Each morning, Malathy Joan went to the window in her pale cotton nightgown to watch the land appear. The first sight burst forth like tongues of fire, the colors so brilliant they looked to leap across the mountains until the trees put forth incandescent leaves. The earth spouted violets and riots of climbing roses. In the vegetable garden, peppers ripened near the burgeoning tomato vines. Malathy felt the wooden floor warm beneath her bony toes. Her eyes opened, the gold there suddenly stunning in the dawn. Her heart offered thanks. Her hope had put down deep roots and now was thriving all across the landscape.

She tended her garden with care. She went to it in her gray cardigan and overalls, her hair braided down her back. She weeded and hoed and picked the fruits of her labor. But it often seemed as though she needed only to put forth her hands, and the tomatoes would drop into her palms. The flowers bloomed unceasingly, and the vegetables birthed and birthed.

In turn, she made pepper relish and bread and butter pickles. She made salads with fresh herb dressings and vegetable soups. There was so much food that she took to leaving jars and covered plates on doorsteps in the town. Some would not eat the food, believing it to be unwholesome. But those who ate once from Malathy Joan's plates would look sorrowfully at their own Monday night suppers, wondering when they would next taste the food from heaven. Their stomachs pawed about inside them like a begging dog, panting, dripping with desire.

Always the Greenberry house smelled fragrant, of wood and flowers and fresh-baked bread. But the most pervasive odor in all the house was that of lilacs. It drifted as a vague perfume scented most strongly in the backs of closets or the bottoms of drawers. Malathy Joan owned no sachets. Neither did lilac bushes grow near the house. Nevertheless, lilac flavored the air, and hints of it crept into the curtains and the sheets and even the food Malathy prepared. Whenever the smell reached her, she felt her shoulders ease, and her arms take on new life. In those days, the stranger woman had no questions. She had come home, and the lilacs smelled to her of contentment and grace.

She walked through the rooms, and pieces of memory would show them-selves like a soft glow. She remembered pale blue curtains in that kitchen window. She remembered a sewing basket beside the rocking chair, and her fingers wandered to the silver pendant on its silver chain. She was not afraid to remember these things that she had never seen. She knew the Greenberry house as she knew her old name, left behind in the cruel city. But her rememberings of the house were clearer now, stronger. They came with noises, sometimes. And, after she had lived in the house three weeks, they came with people.

One morning after breakfast, as she cleared away the table and began to wash the dishes, she first saw Jess Greenberry. Malathy's hands were in the warm, soapy water, and she was cleaning down inside a glass. She turned the dishrag around and around and made her weird humming noises. She caught a glimpse of movement in the window, perhaps a bird eating seed in the birdfeeder outside. So she lifted her head and saw there in the window a face looking back at her. She thought at first her eyes met her own image. Then she caught her breath, and she knew it was the reflection of another woman's face, there beside her own.

She did not drop the glass. She stiffened, pressed her lips tight together. A large, white space opened up in her chest, tingling. She almost turned her head before she thought it best to keep still.

Standing there barefoot, the hem of her dress against her ankles, Malathy Joan looked at the faces she saw in the window. She saw her own face, long and narrow and angular. The other woman's face, to the right of hers, was rounder, with a short nose and a quaint chin. The eyebrows arched like question marks penned in a delicate, flowing script. The hair had been swept up like a Gibson girl's, soft and full with a few stray locks curling around her ears. It was a pretty face and looked as real as Malathy's own. The woman even blinked her eyes like a living creature.

But the eyes did not live. They looked flat and held a strange luster like the glass eyes of a china doll. Malathy could not tell their color. The strange eyes blinked, looking dully at the window.

Malathy felt her heart fall. "Hello, Jess," she said softly, in her strangled voice.

The other woman's eyes shifted towards her and began to widen. The cold light in them opened. The woman's face did not change, but the eyes widened until they were shrill and huge. The lips parted. Malathy felt something chill and damp brush against the back of her neck. Then the face was gone.

Several long minutes later, Malathy stood out on the back stoop, the dishrag balled tight in her hand and suds dripping between her fingers. She did not remember opening the back door or walking into the sunlight.

"I didn't even give my name," she murmured.

She meant the house for peace. She picked it from the vine. She opened doors and windows to let it warm the wooden floor. Malathy Joan had come to bury the dead, to leave them sleeping up on Sumac Hill where they belonged. In those days, she thought only to befriend the spirit of Jess Greenberry and so to ease a wandering soul from wandering.

Another time, Malathy was sleeping beneath her white chenille bedspread when she felt something tug at the covers. She roused a little, slowly, when the bedspread suddenly jerked away. Though the house had never been cold, the air in the bedroom was turning chill. She sat up at once and saw, traced upon the darkness, a woman's shape in an icy silver light.

Malathy crossed her arms in front of her for warmth. She did not reach for the bedside lamp. "I'm cold, Jess," she said quietly. "Have you never been cold?"

There was a soft sound, like gentle bursts of breath. The bedspread dumped across Malathy's legs. When Malathy pulled at the spread to cover herself, she smelled lilacs. The silver shape had faded into the dark.

After that, Jess Greenberry came every day to the house for many days. In the beginning, she came alone. She sat in the rocking chair and turned her face when Malathy passed, the lips pursed with something like amusement. Another time, Jess stood in the kitchen, her hands on her hips. Catching Malathy's eye, she raised her forefinger and placed it to her mouth. There seemed almost a smile there. At midnight, at the back door, Jess beckoned to someone outside, someone who was no longer there.

Then one night, Malathy woke to see Jess pacing the bedroom floor with a young child in her arms. Though Malathy could see the shape of Jess in painstaking detail, down to her bare toes, the child was a silver blur, without face or distinct features of any kind.

"Will the fever break?" Malathy asked.

Jess looked at her over the child's head and nodded.

The next morning, Malathy found the whole family seated at her kitchen table for breakfast. Jess had braided her hair and wound the braids about the top of her head, but all that Malathy could see of the other figures were grey, hazy clouds. The larger one must have been Saul Greenberry, and those were the three little children, the smallest sitting in Jess's lap and beating its hand soundlessly on the table. Malathy wondered what they said to one another. She wished for ears to hear.

Most afternoons, Emmy came up to the house, and Malathy met her on the front porch with a glass of lemonade. Emmy came in snowboots and a heavy coat. She hurried up the path through the garden. It was as beautiful as she had known it would be. Each day that she raced up the slope to the bursting, flaming colors growing about the house, she wanted to catch it all in her arms and drink it through her skin. She wanted it to turn to magenta inside her. She wanted it to shout aloud the rejoicing, to tell her of the calling. After all, Jesus was the gardener on the day of resurrection and would be walking, walking there among the brightness. The dark whispers did not wait for her anymore. It was the sorrowful woman waiting for her, and Emmy was not a bit afraid.

They sat on the steps and drank lemonade. Emmy wriggled out of her coat and kicked off her boots. It was too warm up here for those things.

"Where does sadness go?" she asked. "Does it go down into the ground or up into the sky like clouds?"

"I think it goes slowly, the way mountains are worn down into dust," said Malathy Joan. She rested her glass between her knees, one hand curved around the top. "It fades behind us, in the distance."

"Because I don't hear it anymore. It's not crying there in the house, it's all quiet now." Emmy wrinkled her forehead. "Maybe she's gone back to sleep. Do you reckon?"

Malathy's finger traced the circle at the top of the glass. "I think she's waiting."

Emmy did not like that thought. It sounded like a thin ribbon of shadow coiled about the leg of a chair. "What does she want?"

Malathy lifted her head and breathed out slowly. "That's what I wish I knew." There was a quiet look on the Mary Magdalene's face, Emmy thought, like the beauty of holiness. "Have you seen her, then?" Emmy asked. She moved closer to Malathy Joan and hunched forward a little.

"I've been shown things that I don't understand," said Malathy. She looked at the girl who sat beside her. "Does it frighten you, to talk of her and think of her here?"

Emmy leaned toward the stranger woman, her eyes earnest. "It doesn't bother you any."

A thin, unhappy smile came over Malathy's lips. "It bothers me very much that she's not where she should be. But, no, I'm not afraid."

"I've heard it sometimes, the whispers, and I don't like it a bit. I don't hear them now, though." Emmy turned and looked at the open doorway. Then she turned back to Malathy Joan. Emmy's eyes were shining in her broad, sweet face. "You'll help her, won't you?" She wanted to wrap her arms around the woman and rest her head in the bony lap.

Malathy drew a long breath. "I believe so."

The woman sat so straight there upon the stone step, her long hair black as shadows among the winter trees. Emmy's throat moved. There were no words to say, only the joy of knowing, and it burst through into her most secret place. She clasped the woman's arm with both hands.

"There are many places like this, Emmy," said Malathy Joan. Gently, she freed her arm and wrapped it around the soft, fragile child. "In the city, there are streets that run to buildings that gape onto caverns of everlasting fire. There are bodies always standing and eyes cracked with blood, eyes that never sleep." Her slender hand pressed against the girl's shoulder. "And sometimes a person must walk through those streets and bear blessing in her arms. For no place must be untouched."

Emmy crumpled against the stranger woman. How, how she wanted a calling of her own. Curling up her body, the girl let herself be warmed by the sunshine and the garden flashing like a prism and the flecks of gold in the stranger woman's eyes.

Jess never walked when Emmy visited the house. Neither did Jess walk when Noah came to supper, though Malathy herself did not know when that would be. The first she would know of his coming would be a noise on the front steps and then a knock on the front door. The knock never came at the back door and came even if the door stood open. Malathy Joan would wipe her hands on her apron and call out her welcome.

Then the door creaked, and she heard the sure, even tread of Noah's boots on the wooden floor. He hung his jacket by the front door and put his hat on the low table in the front room as he passed. Then he stood in the kitchen doorway.

"Evening," he said and walked to the cabinet, without waiting for her answer. He began setting down plates and glasses for the supper table.

She was glad when he came. When he did not come, though, she found that it was better so, perhaps because the quiet asked more of her on that evening and she needed to be alone with it. She never wondered how he knew.

"Hello, Noah," she said. She took off her apron and hung it on its peg. "It's good to see you." And it was. She turned to look at him.

He glanced at her and nodded. "Always satisfied to catch sight of you, myself."

Then they would sit down to supper. There was plenty to share. They would hand bowls and butter knives to one another and talk, though sparingly, of what their hands had done that day. Afterwards, they washed and dried the dishes together, and then Noah would linger awhile, often by the fire in the front room, before heading back down the hill to his own home.

Noah never spoke of Jess but once. That night, when Malathy stood to clear the table, she mentioned that the house had been strangely quiet that day.

Noah looked up at her with his hard, black eyes. "I reckon that's how the place was meant to be. There's those wouldn't look to know any more."

Malathy stood with her hands on the table.

"This house was meant for living in." Noah looked down where his fork and knife were crossed on his empty plate. "It doesn't seem much use to be dwelling on what's long gone and can't be helped."

"I mean to help." Malathy stood where she was, her hands gripping the table.

Noah's face never changed. He nodded once, still looking fixedly at the place where the fork and knife crossed one another. "I know."

She watched his face. He did know. As ever, he was unafraid of her, and he believed her. That was not the matter.

"You never spoke of this before," she said.

"I'm what I've been." His throat tightened. "I didn't reckon on giving you cause to doubt me."

The gentleness of his voice made her sad. "I know you, Noah," she said.

His eyes wandered to the light sprinkling of crumbs that had fallen from the bread basket. The basket was empty now, the cloth crumpled. "These last days have been troubling me. But it's not on account of laying awake and wondering if Mrs. Greenberry is walking here."

Malathy heard him now. She wanted now to say far different things. She let herself carefully back down to her seat.

"She can walk if she will," said Noah. He never took his eyes from the table. "The ground up here can grow like a greenhouse all winter long. I've got no quarrel with any of it." He paused, and then the quiet words came, slowly, from the stern gash of his mouth. "But I built for you. And I didn't mean to shut you in here for Mrs. Greenberry or anybody else to be troubling you."

Her fingers still curved about the edge of the table. The feel of the wood pierced her through and through. "I'm safe with her," she said. "I'm quite safe here."

He didn't answer. She saw the lines tighten around his mouth.

"You needn't be afraid for me here," she said. Her hands ached with an unfamiliar pain.

He waited, considering. Then he reached for his empty plate with both hands and stood. "My dreams have been right troublesome these days," he said and turned to carry the plate away.

That was all. He said no more of Jess Greenberry, that night or for many nights after. The questions that stirred about Malathy's heart, causing her to wonder, soon blew away with the perfume of lilacs. Though her large, solemn eyes saw deep and clear, she little heeded what in many ways she knew for the truth, that to look always behind her was to keep the past alive always, that it is said only the dead bury the dead.

In early December, there happened a night like most any other. She and Noah ate spaghetti with her homemade sauce and then went out to sit on the porch. In the shadow of Sumac Hill, the air was warm, the flowers bursting with scent. Even from where she sat, with her feet resting on the stone step, she could smell roses in the dark.

"There's a good fishing place I know," said Noah late into the evening. "I keep a few things there, a tent and a boat in a little shed."

She listened. A cricket sang nearby.

"I've seen deer there many a time and once a fawn. The wild creatures are trusting there." He shifted beside her in the dark. She could hear him move.

"You can follow that river back into the mountains, back to the place where things begin."

The stars were cast upon the darkness above like ten thousand grains of sand. Some of those stars had burned themselves out long ago, Malathy thought, and only that last light trailed behind the stories of their existence. The thought bowed down her spirit, though she sat tall and bony and elegant on the wooden porch of her house.

"When the weather turns fair again," said Noah, slowly, "I thought I might take you over there, if you've a mind to see it."

She remembered the snow down in the creek bottom. She regretted winter.

"I would like that very much," she said.

In the silence, the moment lingered. It spread out from her words like bright circles on a dark river. It was a moment for waiting, and she waited. She thought he, too, waited, hesitant, considering. She turned her face towards him.

"I'd better get on," he said. He gathered himself as though he readied to stand.

The waiting left her, then, as if it were a long breath from the bottom of her lungs. She felt the unfamiliar sting.

"I've been glad of your company," he said. His right hand reached for hers, spread there on the good, sturdy wood.

"You're always welcome," she said. She gripped his hand in return. "Good night, Noah."

She had waited, and it had not come. But she was glad of his slow, careful voice and knew that this treasure, the company they shared, was the richest of all that she laid by. No moths, no thieves, could corrupt it.

As she watched him walk away through the garden, she looked through the darkness and tried to see that river which sprang from the hidden beginnings of things. That would be blessing indeed, to see where the fawns came shyly through the trees and turned their living, liquid eyes upon those who passed. Her lips smiled into the night.

That was the night the star fell. Most folks never saw it. They had shut their windows and doors against the star-shining icicles and the shimmering snow. But Noah glimpsed it as he walked through Beulah Creek, the houses pale as breath. Emmy beheld it from her window as she held a purring Pumpkin in her arms. She made a wish. Grandma Barnes caught sight of the sudden streak upon the dark and felt a shudder through her body. Her dog barked. She knew what it was, a burning bit of rock, but it looked to her of times and things that did not please her any. Many times in the days to come, she would remember from long before the low scuttling along the bottom of her soul, like the claws of crawdads, the secret power of knowing. Then, as now, she did not know what she would do with such a dangerous thing. She reckoned only that it would be long, long, before Beulah Creek again knew peace.

That night, Malathy Joan was rising from the steps to go back into the Greenberry house. Her fingers touched the silver pendant, pressed the place where the tiny bars crossed. She saw the star fall and thought it beautiful as it trailed across the sky.

FIRE

I

Down in Beulah Creek, Noah Carpenter dreamed. He stood in snow that piled to his knees and looked up at the sky. He waited for something. The night showed him nothing but a thick darkness without moon or stars or the lights of houses.

All at once, a loud roar came from the sky, as though the mountains tore down all around him, and the earth shook. He staggered but did not fall. The weight of the snow kept him upright. Alarmed, he lifted his head to see what had happened. The trees high on Sumac Hill burned. The fire climbed up the trees to the bottom of the sky, and the sky above the hill turned a rich red. The beat of his blood knocked powerfully against his chest. But he could not otherwise move. The snow gripped his legs and crushed down around his feet. Knowing her danger, he could do nothing but stand there the whole night through and watch the wood and the house below it fall to ashes.

However, on the night the star fell, in her house overlooking the town of Beulah Creek, Malathy Joan slept untroubled until day. From her purple sleep, she awoke much later than usual to find herself shivering beneath her covers. She sat up, pulling the chenille bedspread taut towards her and wrapping herself in it. Jess Greenberry stood in the room. The woman faced the far wall, and her fingers deftly wove and twisted and pinned her hair up onto her head. The mirror was not to be seen.

"Good morning, Jess," said Malathy Joan.

Jess looked over her shoulder. The smile on her face was vague and secretive before it melted away with the rest of her.

Malathy rose slowly and stretched up the covers. She pondered and breathed the lilac poignance of the lost woman's life.

But when Malathy Joan walked into the front room, she became a little startled to see Jess Greenberry again, in the rocking chair and rocking it violently, looking out the window, her body tense. At Malathy's approach, the woman rose in a rush and went to the shut front door.

"Where are you going?" Malathy asked.

Turning her head, Jess smiled the same cunning smile. But this time she beckoned to Malathy Joan.

So many days of trusting had passed that Malathy stepped forward. "Are you waiting for someone?"

Jess opened the front door and disappeared in the sunlight.

Marveling, Malathy walked to the door and stood with her toes and face and arms in the bright morning. The flowers glowed as though the warmth of the day radiated from their colors. She thought of the pendant and chain still closed up safely in her treasured box. She thought of cutting flowers for her breakfast table, then lingered in the doorway sunshine awhile longer. In the glory of the morning, she turned her face to the sky in prayer and felt the hues of the blossoms shine upon her body.

She left the doorway and crossed to the kitchen for the shears. She had no sooner entered the kitchen than she felt her lungs turn to ice. Jess stood at the back door, unpinning her hair. The woman was naked. Her dress had crumpled to a heap at her feet, and she moved languidly, heedless of the pink tips of her breasts, the curls between her legs. She pulled free the last pin, and her chestnut hair fell down to her waist. Glancing over at Malathy, she smiled the third time, a smile that hinted of death. Her eyes shrieked with a cruel, glassy light, and then she was gone.

Malathy watched where the woman's eyes had faded into silence. The cold crept slowly into her hands and feet, and a deafness began to seethe in her ears. She had felt much the same when Noah told her of his troubling dreams. Then, as now, the feeling disturbed her as much as what she had learned. She took up the shears with hands that trembled only a little.

Once on the front porch, she came down the steps with hesitance, unsettled. Her cotton nightgown clung to her thighs and brushed against her ankles. Blades of grass nudged her feet as she passed. Blood tingled in her fingers. She walked among pansies and marigolds and tiger lilies. She turned towards the rosebushes and the snapdragons with her hand outstretched, grasping the shears.

It was hair, spread out upon the ground, that she saw first, hair the color of sunlight, the color of corn silk. Then she saw a hand, an arm, the small of a back, and realized that someone lay sprawled on his face in the midst of her garden.

The shears fell from her fingers. She crashed through flower stalks and dropped to a crouch beside the motionless figure.

She saw his ripped, faded blue jeans. She saw the rags and ribbons of white fabric that he wore for a shirt. She touched the small of his back with her hand.

"Are you living?" she whispered.

The body did not stir. She felt his wrist, and it beat a dim, dark rhythm upon her fingertips.

Carefully, she rolled him over as gently as she could. He had the most beautiful face she had ever seen. The shock of it pinched her throat until she drew down raw air. She saw the light of it and its firm, full shapes. The sight brought sharp things to her memory, beautiful things she had known and the face of one she had shared them with. He looked so very young.

Then she saw where she touched him and gasped. Blood oozed from a terrible wound. It spattered across his chest, his stomach.

Her breath came in bursts and shots of pain. He would not die at her door. But she did not know how she could take her hands to go for help, to go for anything, and leave him there. So she knelt, thinking what to do, bending over the young man as he bled, while her legs ached to take her away.

Then she heard the sound of feet coming quickly through the garden. She recognized who it might be, marauders come to tear him further, and snatched up the shears as she leaped from the ground. Still she hurried towards the noise, hoping for help. Her gown caught and ripped upon the stalks as she went.

But it was no marauder who walked her land. It was Noah Carpenter who had come up to the Greenberry house. As soon as he had awakened that morning, he had pulled on the clothes he folded on his chair the night before. His dream would not leave him. He could still feel the terrible uselessness of his hands, the dark, sick misery in his chest. He had shaken his head at his own foolish faithlessness as he put on his boots, but, anyhow, he meant where he was going and had set out anyway.

He reached the sunny summer lawn of the Greenberry house with its magnificent tangle of garden. He saw the front door standing wide. He was walking more briskly through the flowers and vegetables and was just set to call her name, when Malathy Joan came darting from among the lilies. Stalks snapped about her, and her hair flew like dark thoughts.

"Noah!" she said. "I need your help."

She carried a pair of shears, and he saw a stain like blood upon her white gown. His lungs froze into a block of cold, terrible certainty.

Then he was moving toward her. He did not know what had come to her, what the work of his hands had caused to happen there. He felt nothing but an immense, crippling sadness.

He reached her as she pelted to a stop, her face stricken. He seized her shoulders and meant to take her from that place.

"No, don't," she said. She looked at his eyes and could not believe what she saw there, how fiercely he regarded her. "This isn't my blood, Noah, I'm not bleeding. She hasn't hurt me. No one here has hurt me."

Still he gripped her. The silver pendant was gone from her chest, he had seen that straightaway. "Tell me what's wrong here," he said.

"I need your help for someone else," she said, and her breath came hard between her words. "He's hurt, he's in the garden, and he's barely alive. I don't know how he came there, Noah, but something must be done for him."

Noah looked past her now, frowning towards the lilies. He swallowed against the misgiving that began to rise from the bottom of his stomach. It tasted ill, thick and yellow.

He loosed her and walked by, back towards the place from which she ran. She came close behind him, for the plants crowded too near for her to walk alongside. Noah felt smothered by their presence and drew off his wool jacket.

He stopped where the broken creature lay, a gangly boy of nineteen, twenty, who was sprawled upon his back. He saw the dark blood welling from the boy's side and turned it over in his mind, what the boy was doing there, what could have gashed him open so. He did not like to think of someone prowling in the night through the mountains with Malathy Joan asleep in the Greenberry house, at the farthest edge of the settlement.

"Should we move him?" she asked.

Noah knelt beside the young man to look at the wound. "We ought to bind this up quick."

"I'll bring something for it." Malathy Joan turned and ran for the house, pushing leaves aside and skirting low clumps of flowers.

She raced onto the porch and sprinted through doorways and into her room. She jerked open a dresser drawer and snatched the first cloth she saw, a neatly-folded bedsheet. The smell of lilacs choked in her mouth. Her eyes smarted as she thought of what was happening just beyond her front door. She had never seen such a beautiful face as his.

She gathered up the bedsheet and bore it back out into the sunshine. She knelt beside Noah and helped him rip the cloth apart with hands and garden shears. They bound the young man's side as well as they knew.

"What do you suppose has done this to him?" Malathy asked.

Noah shook his head. "It didn't mean him any good," he said. He leaned back and drew his arm across his brow. "I don't know as he ought to lie out in the sun. We maybe ought to take him indoors."

"We'll put him on the bed," said Malathy Joan.

Together they carried the limp body into the house and then into her bedroom. The young man groaned as he was laid on the bedspread. His face was slowly falling to ashes.

"He's going to need more help than we've given him," said Noah. He hesitated a moment. "I'll go down and see what I can bring back up again."

She nodded. She watched how the light flickered in the young man's face.

"I'll come as quick as I can," said Noah. He turned to go. "Take care who's at the door."

She heard the tread of his boots as he crossed the floor in the front room and went out onto the porch. He shut the front door behind him. She lingered there at the young man's bedside, uncertain what was best to do.

"What can I do for you?" she said. That was what she wanted to know.

He stirred then. Wearily, he shook his head, his eyes closed. "Send them away," he whispered.

"There's no one here but me," she said. And then, with a vague shudder in her chest, she thought of Jess standing naked at the back door, letting down her hair.

"Don't let them find me," he said. The young man's eyes came open. In the pallor of his face, they were achingly alive, the colors in them shifting like the ever-changing sea. "Please. They have such terrible, thorny fingers . . . ."

His hand moved across the bedspread as though he reached for her. She grasped his hand, understanding only the fear in his voice, the earnestness in his eyes.

"I won't let them near you," she promised.

He closed his eyes, and the tension eased from his face.

"You're safe here," she said, even as she remembered Jess in the front room, rocking, waiting, nervous, peering out the window. "And Noah's gone to bring you help."

"Where am I?" Though the young man barely murmured, his voice carried a resonance, a melodic quality, which gave his words extraordinary texture.

"This is Beulah Creek." She sat on the edge of the bed. "You're in my house." The trace of a smile flowed over his face.

"You can call me Malathy Joan," she said. "It's all the name I have now."

His head moved slightly, like a nod. He winced. "I'll be . . . Addison here."

She heard too many things in his words that she wanted to know. She rose from her seat on the edge of the bed. "Are they following you?" she asked.

He rolled his head from side to side. "But they look for me all the same."

Her eyes lifted quickly to the bedroom window. The sun scattered benison among the zinnias still, but shadows now roamed where she did not know, in the woods behind the house, perhaps, wielding terrible weapons. They had slipped away from the city and found their way to her, to Addison.

"Is there no way to flee them, then?" she asked. Her heart sank inside her like the setting of some warm jewel of a star.

Addison looked very pale there upon the chenille bedspread, his face crumpled as the pillow where his head lay. "I think not," he said.

She did not want to speak such darkness. She did not want to remember the days she had spent with her old name, for her pendant was out of reach, closed in its box in the other room. She wished very much to go and clasp the chain about her neck, so she would not feel herself so porous, so she could hold its silver in her fingers, but she feared to leave the bedside, to return and find the young man's breathing gone. She felt the stir of old troubles from the bearded mire at the bottom of moving waters. She wanted Noah to come back.

As the young man lay broken on Malathy Joan's bed, Grandma Barnes went about her own morning down in Beulah Creek. She switched on her radio to listen to the Earth and Sky program. She could not get her body about as well as she liked anymore, but she could still move her mind and rather liked to hear about the far reaches of dark, where rock and ice moved about in silence and nothing lived. She untwisted the bread bag with her sagging, puckery hands to get some slices for toasting in the oven. She listened to the talk as she placed the bread on the baking sheet and spread the slices over with butter.

A firm knock came then at her front door. The dog started barking. She put down the bread, displeased.

"Hold on there!" she called as loudly as she could.

She wiped her hands down her apron and took up her cane. She went to the door, where the dog stood before it and made loud sounds at whoever might be outside. From the shape she could tell through the curtained window in the door, it was a man. "Hush now, and get out of my way, dog," she said. The dog stopped barking and went to the rug by the front window. Grandma Barnes didn't bother to move the curtain to look before she unlocked and opened the door. No one that she would find on her front steps would surprise her.

Noah Carpenter stood in the sudden swirl of cold with his hands pushed deep in the pockets of his wool jacket. He seemed tense standing there, though his face was never simple to see. Grandma Barnes approved of Noah most days, for his thinking was thorough and clean and sober, his ways tidier than most.

His grandparents, Abel and Irene, had been honest, hardworking people. He was a good man, as men went.

"I don't reckon you've come for breakfast," said Grandma Barnes.

He shook his head. "No, ma'am. I've come to trouble you. I'm sorry for it, but I don't see any way else. You'll know what's to be done."

She saw his van parked in the gravel by her front door. She saw the swirling snow that went spinning slowly to its soft landing. The burning rock she had seen last night would not come to rest so gently. She wondered where it had gashed into the earth.

She squinted up at Noah and wrinkled her eyebrows. "What if I don't like the sort of trouble you've brought me?"

"I can't say as I like it myself," he said.

She nodded, drawing up her mouth as she heard him. "So I suppose the trouble's up there," she said. "In that place where she's got no business."

"Well, now, it's her house," he said. "Some boy has got bad hurt up there."

Grandma Barnes had not the slightest wish to go, misliking what she heard, but Noah was a hard man to refuse, being generally in the right of things.

"Folks are born to trouble," she said. "You'll want me to fetch my bag, I reckon."

She turned then, her cane heavy against the floor, to go to the drawer where she kept her satchel. From its watch by the window, the dog looked carefully at Noah. The carpenter looked back at it likewise.

Some time later, Malathy Joan heard the sound of an automobile pulling up at the far edge of the garden. She slipped to the bedroom doorway to meet whoever came, for she believed it to be Noah. But the front door opened, and it was Grandma Barnes who walked into the house, the sound of her cane a slow, ominous tread upon the floor.

The old woman saw Malathy and clucked her tongue. "My, you're a pretty picture this morning."

Malathy Joan remembered now her thin, pale gown, her hair unkempt, her body unwashed. She reached quivering fingers for her silver pendant, but her neck was bare. "I'm glad of you here," she said.

Noah came in after Grandma Barnes. He carried a small, battered satchel. "Is he still living?" he asked.

Malathy nodded. "He's spoken a little."

Grandma Barnes thumped steadily towards the bedroom door. "I reckon he's in there?" She did not wait for answer but stepped and looked in at the young man lying on the bed. She hissed. She pressed both hands to the head of her cane. "Why did you do this?" she said, her low voice shaken.

Malathy Joan started to say she could never have done such harm to him, so beautiful. "Have we done wrong to move him?"

Grandma Barnes narrowed her eyes at Malathy. "You shouldn't have brought me here. Neither one of you."

"It hardly seemed right to let that boy die in her yard," said Noah.

Grandma Barnes turned then and looked at him. "It would seem so to you, no doubt," she said. She stretched out her gnarled, blue-veined fingers. "I'll need that bag."

Noah handed the satchel toward her, and she grabbed at the handles.

"You can keep out of the way," said Grandma Barnes.

Malathy Joan did not remember how she crossed the floor, but she sank onto the couch as the old woman walked firm-footed into the bedroom and banged the door closed. Malathy shivered.

"I didn't want to see this any more," she said. The words ached in her mouth.

Noah took a slow step towards her. His face was stern.

"The city ran with blood," she said. She bowed her head and spoke against her hands. "The stones drank it. The people drank it. And I drove away from that place."

Noah lowered his eyes. "You might ought to come down from here," he said.

"I don't fear this house," she said, lifting her face. "I don't fear anyone in it."

There were creases in Noah's forehead. She could hear the keen edge of his silence.

"Something hurt that boy," he said at last.

The quiet curdled a little. They stayed unspeaking for a time, Noah standing by the fireplace, his hand spread upon the mantel, and Malathy seated on the couch. She felt the morning darkened. She knew she needed to rise and take the silver chain from its box, but the edges of her sight drew slowly in towards her, and she found it harder and harder to move.

The bedroom door rattled then. Grandma Barnes came out and pulled it to a crack behind her.

"Will he live?" Malathy Joan laid large, careful eyes upon the old woman.

Grandma Barnes sniffed. She leaned her head to one side.

"It won't matter what I've done, however it goes. You'll look after him, no doubt. There's salve on the dresser, and I'll send you another when that's gone." She started across the floor to be gone from the house. "I reckon a beast got him."

Malathy Joan stared where Grandma Barnes walked. She realized anew the terrible brittleness of vessels, vessels of earth, vessels of blood.

"I'll come back," said Noah. He looked where Malathy Joan sat. "I'd be glad of sitting with him tonight, or maybe you'd rather watch awhile and give over in the morning."

"I can watch him however long he needs," she said. "Thank you, Noah." Addison was the work that had come to her, and she would be faithful in his care, atoning for the death of one she had once loved, whose face, less beautiful, was yet reminiscent of his.

Noah hesitated, wanting to say something more. He thought of boughs that sighed to breaking. He gave a short nod. He said, "I'll leave you to manage then."

He turned and followed Grandma Barnes. Several moments later, still sitting on the couch, Malathy found she had not said goodbye.

The people of Beulah Creek slept safely, dreamily that night. Some mumbled from their beds that a strange young man had been mauled by a bear. His wounds pasted with salve and bandaged, he had found refuge in the Greenberry house. No one quite believed in him. Many saw his face in their dreams as though it were just beyond their remembrance, but only Grandma Barnes had truly seen it before. She did not know how it had come about, but Lucien Brown had been dead better than eighty years, and yet the young man wounded in the stranger woman's garden wore his face. With a Bible beneath her pillow, she banished it firmly from her sleep.

II

The first night that Addison lay shattered on Malathy Joan's bed, the snow fell hard on Beulah Creek. The crush of white covered soil and stone, breaking branch and obliterating road in a sweep of wind. It could almost have been that the mountain slopes themselves slid free and came rushing and rumbling into the midst of the town, bearing down the magnitude of years.

Most who lived in Beulah Creek struggled to keep upright. They put their eyes upon the bright, delicate shapes of trees in their living rooms, strung with colored lights that blazed suddenly, briefly, in the dark. They thought of the heaping snow on rooftops, the creaking of timbers. Perhaps, at any moment, the world would fall upon them. They could not find words to speak of this, only they fingered the shining packages and thought them beautiful. People shook their heads and did not see how it could last, the small, perfect magic sheltered precariously beneath the boughs of trees dead and undead.

Though winter did not menace up at the Greenberry house, the dark bumped about the rooms and creaked against the floor, so that Malathy Joan could not sleep. She went to the mantel and took up the little silver cross and circle. She stretched her long body on the couch and watched the shadows creep about the walls, gnashing their teeth and fumbling towards her with their hands. She pulled the blue afghan over her legs and waited for the dawn. She listened through the night and heard even the soft moan of boughs in the wind, but Addison did not cry out.

Towards morning, she slipped to the bedroom door. She felt the crispness in the air before she saw it shimmering like ice about the figure of Jess Greenberry.

The ghost woman bent over the bed. Her long, chestnut hair glowed about her shoulders.

Malathy Joan stepped nearer. "Don't wake him," she rasped. "He might be frightened to see you."

Jess lifted her head and put a finger to her lips. Her other hand brushed the young man's forehead. He stirred fitfully.

"Jess . . . ." Malathy felt something twist in her throat. "Please stop."

Jess shook her head in contradiction, smiling. Strands of brightness curled from her like smoke until her form drifted into the dark.

Malathy Joan stood and looked at the emptiness that Jess Greenberry had left behind, as the purple smell washed against her face. She went to the kitchen. She lifted a chair from the kitchen table and carried it into the bedroom, where she placed it softly on the floor. There she sat until she could see Addison's face formed by the morning light. All the while, her hand rested against the delicate weight of silver to hold her hide upon her bones. She reached to keep herself whole.

As soon as Addison could remain wakeful enough to tell her more than his most pressing need, she told him of the other woman who wandered the house. She did not want him to come to that knowledge suddenly, on his own, for he was weak and hurting and wary of enemies he did not name.

"Jess Greenberry lived here many years ago and walks here now, sometimes," she said.

She watched to see dark fear fall upon his face, but he did not seem disquieted, only curious. "What does she want?" Addison asked. The skin wrinkled above the bridge of his nose. He moved, sitting forward a little, and the covers rustled. "Does she break things, take things? Does she try to frighten you?"

She wondered what Addison might have broken and taken during the days of his life. "I suppose she wants someone to remember her, to learn what became of her. Perhaps she needs someone to help her to peace."

Addison nodded. "And you help her because you need to. Because it isn't a strange thing to you, to be haunted."

He recognized some part of her past wounding, she saw. In this they shared a bond, for both of them had known brokenness. "And you," said Malathy Joan, "you are hunted by evil things."

He frowned. "Am I?"

She looked at him. "You spoke it to me, the first day you came here."

He smiled. "Did I say that? I must have said many strange things, nonsense things, as badly as I was hurting then. But it's true in a way, I suppose," he said, and his smile was gone. He turned his face so that he looked towards the uncurtained window. Unsettled as she watched, sorrowful for his pain, she let the matter go.

Malathy Joan devoted her time to caring for Addison. She cooked his meals and fed him until he gained the strength to cut his own food and put the fork into his mouth. She put fresh medicine on his wound and dressed it. She helped him to the toilet behind the house and heated his bath water on the stove. Before long, Addison came into the rooms where she worked. He sat sideways in a kitchen chair, one arm wrapped about the chair back. He leaned deeply into the couch, his heels resting against the low table, and he talked. As he returned to his strength, he had more to say. He had moved about often in his young life. He recounted apples and kisses thieved. He remembered bones and windows broken. He opened his hands as he spoke, and she lifted her head from her work to watch him. He would smile then. He raised his eyebrows as though he posed a question. His face was like polished silver, and his smile was white with radiance. She hurt in her throat to think what had come to him. She believed that by pondering his words in her heart, she would come to know the way to help him most.

One night, with the supper dishes washed, they sat together in the front room. Addison sank back into the chenille pillows and stretched out denim legs down the length of the couch. Malathy Joan sat in the rocking chair, stitching at the hem of a skirt that had come unsewn. The quiet did not lie between them long.

"Why do you take such care for me?" said Addison. "You have fed and tended to me, and listened to all my stories."

"Because I have not always taken such care with others or with myself," she said. Her hands pulled the thread steadily. "But once, in the city where I was, someone helped me. Now I've come to give help as I can."

A smile opened in his voice, the curve of lips, the sheen of teeth behind them. "I should like to know something more of you, Malathy Joan."

Her eyes followed the flick and pierce of the needle. These last years had been empty of ears to catch and a heart to hold what she might say. She had hope still of her friend, Noah, if ever he asked her.

"I had another name once," she said. "I let others speak and touch it, in ways I should never have done. I gave it as silver to be tarnished by many fingers."

"It's a hard thing, to survive," said Addison. "If you fight your way through the mire, your clothes are stained beyond help."

She let the sewing rest still in her lap. "No," she said. "Death came where I have gone."

She had traced its red footprint, caught its fanged face in a sliver of mirror. She wished to speak to the young man of what she had learned in the distant city before worse hurt came to him. She believed on the hill high above Beulah Creek, where vegetables grew without season and the cold never came, that she could cast out any demon that might linger in her house. The quiet moved about in the dark places. She smoothed the cloth in her lap.

"I was young when I went to the city," she said. "I looked for different things in that place."

"You're not old now," he said.

A sorrowful smile left her lips almost before it came. "Perhaps not." The hinges of her heart creaked a little. "I found work to do after I arrived there, and a young man ate where I served. He had beautiful hands and used them with pencils, with watercolors. We were lovers for a time." She thought on his name, not so different from that given by the young man before her. It brought her Adrian's eyes and his close, curling hair.

"What became of him?" said Addison, his fingers sinking deep into one of the pillows.

"He drank wine and grew sad, dark in his spirit," she said. "And another man came to the place where I worked."

When she remembered this man, she saw once more the cut that marked where he began and where the space beyond him stopped. She remembered the lines of his clothing, the sharp lines of his form, the lean, taut lines of his movement. She had been drawn by them as though by thick, knotted cords, by commandment.

"I could keep nothing back from him," she said, "not myself, not anything. I went away from Adrian." Turning her head a little, she looked how the glass shaped the lamplight in a warm curve. It spread a simple beauty, one she now preferred.

"My work became different, afterwards," she continued. "The older man traveled between many cities. He kept me in one of them, his wife in another. I knew this. Everything was well-appointed, well-arranged. I owned things." She met Addison's eyes. "I let it be."

Addison dropped his shoulders slightly, the barest shrug. "You let it end," he said.

"It ended," she said. "Adrian died first."

She spoke so that the words she made would not catch her heart with hooks. She touched the silver she carried about her neck.

"I learned of it, how it was, the blood of his veins upon the wall," she said. "And then I carried the older man's child. That, too, ended. Even in such a choice, I could not refuse that man." She felt a dullness in her chest that was a heavy pain. "The time afterwards was black for me. He brought me medicine, his friend wrote it up for me. But still the days dripped with darkness, and then he left. Everywhere I went, I saw people walking like cadavers risen, moving down a sidewalk paved with headstones. I stopped going. I stopped for a long time."

The lamplight flickered. The air shifted in the room. She felt it change.

"That is a bitter story," said Addison. "I understand now, why you've come. You've come to lay the dead to rest."

"I don't fear to remember," she said. "But the power of it will not hold me. I mean to rise above it, what I have left behind. I believe that can be done."

Addison turned his face so that he watched the kerosene lamp. The burning warmed his eyes, and the colors in them leaped bright.

"I knew a man," he said. "He went around the country with a fiddle tucked under his chin, and trouble always stirred up in his wake. It didn't matter where he took his feet. Did he bring the trouble with him, I wonder? Or did the passing of his feet only sift it, make it rise?"

She reached her thumb and forefinger to catch the circle softly gleaming against her blouse. "Trouble does not always follow," she said. "I don't believe it so."

He arched an eyebrow. Light spread across his features. "It matters to you," he said. "To believe." His face was like a window, a mirror that made all things bright and beautiful.

"Yes," she said. She put her fingers again upon the skirt in her lap. The fabric felt gentle as breath against her skin. "It's why I am alive."

Addison raised his left arm to the back of the sofa, his hand cupped slightly. "I am not like you in that way," he said. "Perhaps that is why I come so close to death."

"There can be life in this place," she said.

He shrugged and smiled. "You and I will watch and see."

She creaked the rocker again. She could not say why his dark, smiling words troubled her. He spoke them with full, earnest lips, and she saw light in him that breathed from his skin, that hung in his hair like perfect, shining beads of water. She lowered her eyes and took up her mending. His face and his words lingered within her as a bright shape behind closed eyes. Moving her hand, she bound the severed fabric together with a slip of the thread.

Down the long, tall hill, the people of Beulah Creek stood by their windows, watching the road disappear into the falling, blinding bits of dark. Down that road had disappeared many who had gone to Millsborough to work and had not returned. Each night, Veeny Anderson went to her knees for the Beulah Creek souls trapped and lonesome in the lowlands. For much of each day, Sam and Kenny McGuire, Jack Hendrick, and Noah Carpenter stood in boots and hats and heavy coats in the climbing snow and chopped wood. They carried wood and coal to house after house, where thankful hands stored it against the fearful possibility that the town would be plunged into darkness. In the evenings, Sarah Mullins brought the telephone to the supper table with her children, waiting for her husband's voice to visit them. And always, the high, white sky crumbled across the mountains, the wind stirring trees in their sleep.

Clement Foster was among those from Beulah Creek who had sought refuge in a motel room in Millsborough. Emmy took to sleeping with her pink quilt tugged over her head so she could not hear the emptiness opening all around her. It made a sound like the slow draw and stir of liquid before it began to boil. She felt small with her daddy so far away.

One morning, she could not bear it any more, so Emmy grabbed clothes and pulled them into a suitcase before she had even eaten breakfast. She packed her Bible, too, and a box of cheese crackers, and she gathered up Pumpkin before setting off for the Greenberry house. Pumpkin squirmed as she clutched him, trying to keep him from the cold.

She neared the great, green garden. She walked past beans and peppers and onions. She gazed up at sunflowers that had grown until they might have been trees and now watched the land with giant eyes. She looked away, feeling hot watchfulness upon her skin. Someone waited, she realized, someone she could not see. She had never seen this one, and she did not know what it would be to look. Her heart moved faster, and her head felt dizzy.

She began to run, clumsily, with her head lowered. Only a few moments ago her heart had bounced with joy as she approached the Greenberry house. Pumpkin made a pitiful sound. "I love you, kittycat," she whispered against his fur. He mewed in reply.

She hurried past poppies and chrysanthemums and found herself abruptly at the edge of the garden. She lifted her eyes to the front porch.

First she saw the color of his hair, bright and terrible as lightning in summer dark, falling past his shoulders. She started to shut her eyes. A man stood there, wearing only a pair of faded jeans. She had never seen so much of anyone else in her life. White cloth bands wrapped about the man's stomach. He held a dark pottery mug in his left hand, his right fingers slipped beneath it. He looked out upon the garden. He did not look at her, not yet, but his face was aware. It was brilliant like the diamond song of windchimes, striking notes sweet and strange across the field. It made her throat dry, and her palms wet. She watched because she did not dare to look away.

Then his eyes flashed across her. She flinched. His eyes seemed to come down from the sky, the colors there turning, always moving. There was no place she could go.

"You were here before," he said. His voice was made of falling snow.

Emmy felt the calling. It welled through her, and she could not move. She could only shake her head.

"Not since you've come," she said, her words like phantoms. Yet when she beheld him, she had known always that this one would find her, somehow. She felt her most secret places opening. The man leaned his head to one side, and his eyes watched down, down, down into her. In her arms, Pumpkin struggled to escape. She could feel the tears coming.

Pumpkin yelped and flicked his claws against Emmy's arm.

"Pumpkin!" she wailed. She dropped the cat to the ground. Her heart hurt. The bright blood welled where his claws had gone.

The man smiled. "You don't have to be afraid of me." He spoke as though each word were a many-sided thing, flashing bright. He arranged them so that she could see the best side of all.

Emmy looked on his face, and dark things passed across her heart. She did not want to see him there without his shirt, his hair like white fire. She did not want him to see her with his eyes blue and changing, high and cool as they watched. If she crumpled away, if she turned and ran among the stalks, the giant eyes would search her out.

Malathy Joan came into the doorway. She opened the storm door and walked onto the porch. "What is it, Emmy?" she asked.

Emmy was shaking. "Daddy's down in Millsborough and can't say when he'll be back." Her chin trembled. Her blood still welled from her arm. "I was going to stay home, but the walls got awful empty last night. Can me and Pumpkin come up and stay with you awhile?" Even as she said it, she did not know if she could bear to huddle beneath that man's eyes, to walk anywhere for him to see. She sank and dropped her suitcase. She patted Pumpkin's head, and the cat butted its nose against her hand. She felt castaway, like she should huddle in the woods and weep.

"You know you're welcome here," said Malathy. "You should have come before now."

"Who . . . who is he?" said Emmy, reaching both hands to the cat.

"I'm your friend, Emmy," said the man. His mouth was full of smiling that went down into her heart like gold dropped in deep places where boats were lost. "If you're Malathy Joan's friend, you certainly are mine."

Emmy did not look where the smiling was.

"This is Addison, Emmy," said Malathy. "He's my guest here. He's not so much older than you."

Emmy licked her lower lip. "What happened to him?" she asked. She wondered if a hole gaped in the man's side, a great bloody gorge beneath the bandages.

Malathy came down the steps to Emmy and knelt there in the grass, placing hands on the girl's shoulders.

"He's suffered an accident," said Malathy. "But he's better now. He's resting here."

Emmy gathered the cat into her lap and let herself lean into Malathy Joan. The bony hands shifted, clasped together again against Emmy's back so that the girl was enfolded by arms. Emmy shut her eyes and thought of the most gracious, giving unto that she could imagine. It would open like morning glories, like the rich magenta daybreak, like the stranger woman's hands as she carried the soup tureen to the kitchen table. Again Emmy looked beyond Malathy Joan's shoulder. She saw Addison upon the porch, holding the steaming mug and watching her. She feared to get close to him. She feared to find the thing that had left the chasm in his side.

Malathy Joan loosed the girl and brushed the hair back from Emmy's face, and the soft, milky eyes turned up to look at her. Her heart pinched. She stood, her skirts sighing.

"Come inside," she said. She felt Addison's presence differently now. She had never thought it strange for him to be there, but now Emmy's face tipped open before her and wondered, beholding all that passed. She took up Emmy's suitcase. She had not come to live a secret life in Beulah Creek, and she did not mean to do so now.

She turned to walk back into the house and the day that unfolded. She heard Emmy moving, getting to her feet, and the cat mew. Malathy Joan thought of all her house would hold, a broken boy, a spirit woman, a lost and lonesome girl. She would have to open her hands wide enough to receive them all. She believed it could be enough. She carried Emmy's suitcase up the steps and into the house, passing into the shadowy rooms.

In the nights that followed, Malathy Joan's sleep became restless as it had not been in many a long time. Many mornings she would wake from her pallet on the floor to remember how Jess Greenberry had rocked in the chair by the front window through the night, watching where she lay on the hardwood floor. Sometimes the spirit woman spread one hand across a swollen belly as she rocked. The sight visited Malathy Joan until it became familiar as a dream. She wondered what child it was that would be born.

Once upon waking, she recalled that Jess had stood and rummaged about the mantel, looking through the objects there as though something had been mislaid. Malathy had sat up from the floor. Jess turned sharply and looked at her, a frown on the pretty brow and rosebud mouth. Something was clutched in Jess's hand.

"What have you lost?" Malathy Joan asked her.

Jess shook her head and pointed her finger. Though she could not quite remember, Malathy had thought the ghost woman pointed at her.

III

Noah Carpenter was taking some of Grandma Barnes's salve to the Greenberry house when the power went off in Beulah Creek. That evening when he climbed the hill, he could see the lights burning along the creek bottom where folks went about their lives. He knew those lights, each one, the way he reckoned the Lord knew the stars in the sky and called them by name. Then the town went out upon the darkness. It was a sight to stop him where he stood. He swallowed. He opened and closed his gloves inside the pockets of his green wool jacket. He saw no sense in looking about for signs, going to and fro and chasing after wind. But he figured it was hardly foolish to know what a body was looking at and call it by its name. It would be a bad night. Folks in Beulah Creek would turn cold and near-sighted, bumping into furniture and each other in the bitter dark.

Noah trudged up towards the Greenberry house through the snow. He bent his neck and hunched his shoulders whenever the wind fumbled at his jacket. From the porch of the Foster place, the windchimes called sadly as he passed. They put him in mind of a tiny, lonesome voice he had heard in a dream. He would awaken in the night from grey moments like the trunks of trees tossing in a heavy rain. He would awaken with a thick, knotted feeling in his stomach and could not reason why. Now, with the black mountains pressing down all around him, he pulled his hat lower on his forehead to keep the snow from his eyes. It had been blinding him this while, he realized. He ought to have been by before now.

Soon he reached the place where the sky was watery black and shimmering warm with stars. He heard Emmy singing before he saw her. She was a child of the kingdom ahead of them all, who had come into this world with great misgiving. Ruth Foster had died of bringing her fifteen years before. Emmy was sitting on the front steps, her head drifting to one side, her body rocking back and forth.

"There will be a day, and there will be a day," she sang. "Oh, once there lived a baker man who baked like only bakers can, and so I went to see, la la. The road was full of columbine, buttercups and twining vine. I picked a rose, I stubbed my toe, I burned my hand upon the stove. Oh, Lord, please don't let the rain come back no more."

It was no song that Noah knew. It had a rather shapeless tune, and he figured she was making it up as she went. "Evening, Miss Emmy," he said. He took off his hat as he neared the porch.

Emmy gasped when she saw him. "Oh, no," she said, lowering her head and covering her face with her hands. "You shouldn't have heard me."

"I don't reckon I heard too much," he said, clutching the brim of his hat. He had to take shallow breaths to keep from smelling the garden, rank with sickly, oozing vegetables.

Emmy reached down one of her hands and tugged at the hem of her dress. She was trying to cover her feet with the fabric. She had to lean forward and hunch herself smaller.

"You doing all right? You heard from your daddy?"

"There's no phone up here," she said to her feet. "Daddy's down in Millsborough. I'm doing all right. I come out here mostly."

Noah took off his gloves, folded them together, and stuffed them into his jacket pocket. "You seen Miss Malathy Joan?"

Emmy nodded. "They're in the kitchen."

Noah stopped unzipping his jacket. He looked at the girl who now rested her chin in her hands. "Mrs. Greenberry's in there?"

"She's always in there, I reckon," said Emmy, sadly, shaking her head. "But she hasn't come out today. Malathy Joan's seen her plenty, but I've never seen her."

It was the boy, then, in the kitchen. Noah pulled off the jacket and doubled it over his arm. He knew this, that Emmy was sitting out in the dark by herself, when the kitchen was full of Malathy Joan and her supper. He knew this, too, that it was not right. He did not like it at all. As he climbed the steps, he reached and touched the girl lightly on the shoulder. Emmy slunk sideways from under his hand.

He found the storm door closed, the heavy wooden door open. He stepped inside. The whole house glowed with ruddy light. It smelled like dust and antique cloth. Through the kitchen doorway, he could see Addison sitting at the table in ragged jeans and an unbuttoned, plaid shirt. The young man was looking up at Malathy Joan, talking to her. Malathy Joan was placing her soup tureen on the table. Her hair was braided and wound atop her head like some intricate basket.

Noah let the storm door shut hard behind him. The Fosters' orange cat, Pumpkin, started from sleep beside the hearth. Malathy Joan lifted her head, and her eyes were like nothing but the finest golden dusk across the winter sky. "Noah." She smiled.

"Miss Malathy." He nodded. He set his hat and jacket on the low table as he walked to the kitchen doorway. Addison looked at him with the smoothest face he had ever seen. Noah tried to think where a boy of nineteen, twenty years old, would get such a face. The thought paced up and down, to and fro, and troubled him with its noise.

"It's so good to see you," said Malathy Joan. Her lips were like valleys of shadow in the dimness. "Come in and eat with us." She walked around the kitchen table. She was wearing clothes he had never seen before, a black blouse and long grey skirt with a fringed shawl, the color of mist and lilacs, belted at her waist. The silver pendant was missing from her neck.

He felt a sudden, unreasoning anger. "Emmy going to eat with you?" he asked. "She's sitting out there by herself."

A tremor passed through her eyes. Malathy Joan raised her bony fingers in her familiar gesture, but they never reached the place where the silver circle had always been. "Yes, of course. I'll get her." She walked quickly past him, but he could still see something stricken in her face. "Emmy?" she called as she left the room.

Noah faced the boy, who no longer met his eyes. Instead, Addison was looking towards the floor somewhere beyond where Noah stood.

"You look like you're mending pretty well," said the carpenter.

It was the cat that Addison watched. The cat was trotting towards the table, and Addison watched the animal move. "Hello, Pumpkin," said the young man as though Noah had not spoken.

Pumpkin meowed and hurried closer. Addison leaned his face out over the floor, looking down at the creature. The cat meowed again and wrapped its tail around the young man's ankle. Addison lifted his eyes, then, to Noah's face. "You're Noah Carpenter, aren't you? Malathy Joan told me what a friend you've been to her here."

Noah did not know what came into his heart then, but it felt small and dark with coarse, matted hair. The thing gnawed at the muscle until the taste of salt and iron welled up in his throat.

"I'm grateful to you myself," said Addison.

"Something really tore the hide off you." The taste in Noah's throat would hardly let him speak. Noah walked to the cabinet to take down a glass and plate. "Reckon somebody ought to keep a lookout for that beast."

"There's no beast," said Addison with a rueful smile in his voice. "They're enough. Though I suppose I'm as safe from them here as I'll ever be."

Noah looked at the boy again. He thought first of the prison over the mountains, and then did not like the thought. "You running from somebody?"

Addison's eyes gave Noah a furtive sideways look that was still somehow as cool and smooth as the rest of his face. "You might say that." It was not in Noah Carpenter to dislike anyone. But Noah was beginning to hate Addison with a hatred that was ugly and stinking. He walked behind the boy's chair. He figured it was the eyes that troubled him so, always running away. He could not think on it much, for the small, coarse-haired animal chewed and chewed until he tasted nothing but blood. He laid the plate upon the table and set the glass down beside it. The color of the wood was like honey, clean and smooth and good. He rested his fingertips there.

Malathy Joan returned then with Emmy following her, and they all sat down to supper. No one bothered to say grace. Emmy never took her eyes from her plate. She ate five buttered slices of bread by wringing them into pieces and swallowing them. Addison asked if anyone wanted salt or pepper or some other thing, and Emmy shook her head whether he spoke to her or not. Malathy Joan glanced across the table from time to time. Her face held no peace and the gold of her eyes faded as she looked for Noah. Towards her, there was a darkness, a sternness in him that she had never seen before. She could not fathom it, why he had not come and now he had. She put her fork into cucumbers and thought of days put by like jars full of her garden. She did not know how to open them before him. Noah ate little. Malathy's food tasted bitter in his mouth.

When her plate was finally littered with crumbs, Emmy murmured, "I'm leaving, please." She slid from her seat. Pumpkin made a sound like a question and tried to follow her, but she went out the back door, and it bumped shut in Pumpkin's face. Pumpkin looked at the door. Noah felt the soreness of the day's work weighing upon his bones and was figuring on leaving himself. Nothing there was as it should be.

Malathy Joan stood without a word and began stacking plates.

"Do you need help?" asked Addison. His eyes were beautiful with consideration.

Noah watched as Malathy Joan turned her face towards the young man. She smiled, not unkindly. "You go rest awhile," she said. "I can manage. You aren't wholly yourself yet." She sounded sad and weary.

"Perhaps I've never been myself," said Addison. "But you might persuade me in many things, Malathy Joan, if you keep me long enough." His smile was like secret laughter, and his head moved in an engaging, obliging way. He looked over at Noah and raised his brows as though he had just recognized a friend. "I'll catch you later," he said to Noah. The words sounded odd in his mouth, bumping strangely.

Addison got haltingly to his feet and ambled into the front room. Noah was not sorry to see him go. Turning from the back door, Pumpkin trotted after the boy. Malathy Joan was carrying the plates to the sink, and the cat's tail brushed her long, grey skirt as it went by.

"Emmy doesn't seem right this evening," said Noah. There was a small puddle of soup on the tabletop near his fingers. "She doesn't seem much happy somehow."

"No," said Malathy Joan after a pause. She had watched Emmy huddle in corners, creep away among cornstalks. Her arms had reached for the girl until she no longer knew how best to draw her near. She had come to feel unease beneath the girl's pale gaze, a creeping heat upon her neck, so that when Emmy wandered and took her eyes to some other place, Malathy let her go. She took the dishrag and dipped the plates in the foaming water. "I don't believe Clement will be home for Christmas," she said, and felt a dryness in her throat. "You haven't come in awhile, Noah. I've missed you here."

"Well," he said, looking at her with his harsh, black eyes. "I reckon I've been working. Folks down there are having a winter."

The dishrag went still and limp in her hand. "I suppose they are," she said. She looked out the window. There was nothing but dark upon Sumac Hill, but she shook her head as though she watched the fall of distant, ghostly snow. "I haven't forgotten that much, what the winter can do." The house chilled her sometimes, when the silver shape of Jess Greenberry fell across her, when the air smelled of lilacs in a cold rain.

"It's as bad a one as I've seen. Folks aren't going out, to church or anywhere. Jack doesn't have but a few cans left on the shelves." Noah took his napkin and cleaned the soup spill from the table. "The power went out as I was coming up here."

In her rasping voice to the night beyond the window, she said, "I'm sorry, Noah. I'll bring down some jars." She bent her head and cleaned the plate in her hand. "I've put up more than I'll ever need. I'll come before the week is out. There's plenty here." She had tended to Addison, but she had neglected to be neighbor to others.

Noah looked where his hands were splayed upon the tabletop. "Don't reckon I've seen you without that necklace of yours, not but that once." He still saw it, sometimes, without wanting, the blood smeared on her nightgown as she ran through the garden to him. "There's a lot here I've never seen before." He could not stop the thing gnawing at him, could not stop the sick, smothering feeling it gave.

Malathy Joan stopped moving. Then she reached her fingers up from the dishwater and groped at her neck.

"Oh, God," she whispered. Her words scraped from her throat. Noah heard broken things in them. She turned with her eyes forsaken, dark and trembling. "What's come over me?" Her fingers dripped there onto her blouse.

Noah came out of his chair then, but she rushed from the room, strewing water, before he could move towards her.

He got around the table at last and came through the doorway. He found Malathy Joan standing before the fireplace. She looked into the little wooden box on the mantelpiece. Noah had never seen her eyes so empty. She still held the wet plate. He went to her and took the plate into his hands.

"I can't think where else it could be," she said. The firelight twined like fine gold through the intricate braids of her hair.

"You need help looking?" His hands were well-calloused with years of holding onto things. He'd find this thing if it took years more.

"I put it here," she said with conviction. "The other night . . . ." She touched the box gently with her fingertips.

A hot, wincing anger bit into the soft muscle in Noah's chest. This was what he had figured all along, or something very like it. He had seen sorry, jackleg work in his day, with floors every which way but plumb and doors hung crooked so they could not keep out what belonged out. He reckoned he knew what he was seeing by now when he looked at that boy.

"Maybe somebody's been sticking his fingers where he shouldn't be," said Noah, and he was not sorry to say it.

Her hand slipped, and the box snapped closed. She was startled to hear the hatred in Noah's voice.

"Not you." She turned her head and looked at him. She had never thought this, that Noah did not believe. Something precious shattered inside her, and she felt the pain down to the bottom of her soul. "Not you, Noah. He's alone, entirely alone. Surely you know what that is, to be alone." She would not turn from Addison as she had done from Adrian, leaving him to his own hands. "There's no one unworthy of help," she said, "not my help."

Noah's brow was angry, the turn of his broad mouth almost cruel. It was how his face was made. "Malathy," he said, slowly. "That boy is no account. I won't tell you different just because you want to hear it that way. That boy don't mean you no good, nor Emmy either."

Her neck and shoulders stiffened. "I don't believe you," she said. "I can't, and I won't."

They stood there with dark, unmoving faces. The fire hissed, and the air burned up and fell as ashes between them.

Then Noah put the wet plate on the table. Steadily, carefully, he took the salve from his jacket pocket and set it beside the plate and gathered up his things. She did not dare to watch him. Her eyes were smoking. She heard the even, deliberate tread of his boots across the floor. She could not move, not even as the front door closed softly. She knew she had just lost Noah Carpenter and his faith in her. She had to rest her hand upon the mantel to keep the house from falling down. She did not know how she could stand.

After many long minutes, Malathy Joan groped her way at last onto the porch. She smelled the tomatoes she had not picked and the flowers she had not watered. She saw a void where the creek bottom should be and remembered that the power had failed in Beulah Creek. Up where she lived, the power had never come. Her face stung with sorrow.

"I'm sorry, Malathy." Addison sat cross-legged on the porch with the cat curled in his lap. She only knew him there by the light from the house and the light of the stars.

She shook her head. "You should get to bed," she said. "You're mending yet." She could see nothing, feel nothing clearly, but this, that Addison had not brought this loss to her.

"I'm as well as I've ever been," he said. "I'm not tired, really. You've looked after me completely. No one has ever done for me as you have done, Malathy Joan."

His voice was a comfort to her. She wanted to touch the silver circle at her neck. Her hands shook. "I've got to sleep," she said. Her nights brought her no rest.

"Why don't you go and lie down?" he said. "It could ease you a little."

She had not felt such weariness since leaving her life in the city, the life she had died every day. She tried to remember all she had lost. "I should go and call Emmy," she said. "She gets to strange places these days."

"I'll look for her," he said. "She's a curious little soul, but I think I know where she might be."

Malathy Joan nodded. She could not speak against him. There were no words for it, for she had lost them all, too. "If you wouldn't mind, I would be glad of your help." Her eyes were changed to the dimness now. She saw him stroke the cat in the dark.

"I don't mind," said Addison. "I'll go."

It was true that Emmy had taken to straying farther and farther from the Greenberry house. Though she felt the call of Addison's eyes always, there was nothing Emmy knew to give unto. The voices in the house would try to tell her things, and she covered her ears. Neither did the garden, once so magic and shining, seem welcome to her. It began to smell like something unpleasantly hot and moist. She could not look at her Bible there.

So at first, Emmy would climb a little ways up Sumac Hill behind the house and sit on a large rock. From there, peeping among the trees, she could look down on the Greenberry house and on her own house farther down towards Beulah Creek. She could read her Bible and watch the shadows go laughing and chasing and shifting across the page.

One day, as she looked out at the grey mountains of winter, the thought had come to her of the dead that lay on the summit of Sumac Hill. The thought of them did not frighten her, for there was no emptiness where the dead were, in heaven with Jesus. If she followed them up there, then she would not be alone as she sat. She had curled her fingers about the top of the open book, her palms touching the words. She belonged to the dead upon the hill, and they to her. They were her people. Emmy thought, too, of the Mary Magdalene and her calling, how she lived unafraid with Jess Greenberry in the house.

So Emmy had climbed the hill and sat among the tombstones. It was colder up there, but not without peace, she found. She had leaned her head against the cool stone as though she pillowed against the warm flesh of her kin. All around her stood a frail scroll of iron, scabbed with years, and beyond stood the trees, their shapes fading like time across the mountains. A single, great evergreen stood over her, its roots mingling with the dust.

Emmy listened as dead leaves stirred in the forest. She lifted her hand to touch the stains of moss and age on the stone. She placed her fingers in the grooves of words. She tipped back her head and looked where the trees pointed. She thought what it might be to get to her feet and stretch to the height of the trees. It would be high and dizzy and brighter than ten thousand suns, where the trees climbed, hoping. Her heart would grow full, and all the empty parts of her would shine out forever.

In the days that followed, she returned often to that place. She came when she was glad. She came when she wanted to leave Addison's strange and terrible eyes.

On the night Noah brought salve to the Greenberry house, it was to the graveyard that Emmy fled after supper. She felt hot and queasy and wrapped her arms about herself. She sat until she realized the smoky-sweet smell of green needles about her and the movement of air upon her face. She looked at the tower of dark overhead, the evergreen tree that laddered the space between her and the sky. She closed her eyes and breathed a long time.

"You're not afraid of this place." It was Addison who spoke.

Emmy kept her eyes tight shut, yet she knew the lids trembling.

"That's good," he said. "It's right that you should come here."

He had parted the darkness like stems of grass and moved towards the graveyard. He had come with his eyes and voice of crystal, flashing colored fire. His voice went straight to her brain. She lowered her head.

"These are my folks," she said. "They're at peace with Jesus."

"Are they, now?" he asked.

The emptiness opened in her stomach. She struggled to keep her eyes closed. "Yes," she said. "The Bible says it." The words shook in her mouth.

"Malathy Joan told me that someone walks in her house," he said. He came nearer, limping a little. She could hear the sounds of his walking. "How can that be, I wonder, if that woman is at peace?" The grass moved, and the earth whispered, until he stood very close to her. She heard nothing then but her own blood, swift and hissing.

"I . . . I don't know," said Emmy. "Maybe she likes it there. I never asked her. I don't want to ask her." She had opened her eyes. Her head down, she saw his feet pale shapes in the dark. They made her think of the soft voices that twined through the garden and breathed through the Greenberry house. She wanted to touch Pumpkin.

Then Addison crouched before her. His knees spread to cover everything beyond. "I know why you're here, Emmy."

It did not matter what she said. It did not matter what she did not say. He could see right into her with his eyes of fire, blue-hot. Her stomach rolled and twisted until it opened down into the very bottom of all things. He had learned the most private hope she clasped close. Her voice trembled onto her tongue. "I'm hoping for the calling," she whispered.

"Yes." There was a slender smile in his voice. "You want a word to tell you what will be. A word to say what is yours. That is a good hope for a good, gentle girl like you, Emmy."

Slowly, she lifted her head. The dark places of his face gaped like the emptiness within the mountains. She could not look away.

"There is a power in knowing, Emmy," he said. His voice seemed to come from all around them, from the stars, from the trees, from the ground.

"I would like to know," she found herself saying. Her voice bubbled up in her throat. "There's so much. It's hard to belong here sometimes."

"Do you want to know something?" he said. "I know why that woman rises from her grave and walks."

Her ears would burst from the pounding. Malathy Joan, who lived with the dead, her sorrow a strong magic, had never told such a thing. "How can you do that?" said Emmy. "Know what nobody can, unless you asked her?"

His smile in the dark was soft and twinkling. "I can show you," he said. He stood slowly and walked through the deep blue shadows to Jess's gravestone. He paused there, and Emmy thought he rested his hands upon it. "This is what I know," he said, his back to her.

Emmy scrambled to her feet. The ground was shaking where she stood. "But I never saw nothing like that on her stone," she said.

"But it's here." Addison turned then. She saw the glimmer of his eyes in the night. "Come and see for yourself, since you doubt." There were terrible smiles in his words.

She was frightened to look at him. Still she looked. "It's awful dark to see," she said. Slowly she stepped towards Jess Greenberry's gravestone. She wanted to know, she would know, and this hope drew her forward. The calling would shower upon her shoulders, blooming like summer fields drenched in magenta, and she would bow her head and give thanks. Malathy Joan would thank her, too.

Addison moved aside as she approached. "If you know something true that others cannot see, that will make you fine indeed," he said.

She quivered to know what he thought, and then she stood by him. His body poured against her like rivers of fire, though they did not touch. "Where does it say?" she asked.

Addison's hand snatched her left arm just below the elbow. She gasped. He smeared her hand across the stone. She knew the words her fingers dragged over, what was written there in the bright day. She shook her head hard.

"That don't have nothing to do with Jess walking," said Emmy. "That there says Carried Away, and that means angels taking her away with them to Jesus." But her spine surged with hot shivers. She thought of fire, the Lord's holy fire.

Addison's warm breath twisted fine strands of sound among the locks of her chestnut hair. "But Jess Greenberry did not go with angels," he said. "You know it, and I know. That woman walks because she must, because she never got it out of her, that restlessness without any ease, her body burning, down through the generations it goes." The words scalded where they came against her skin. She could hear teeth in his voice. "I should think you know very well what it means to be carried away, quite carried away."

His voice was silver-white, and everywhere it touched her, she was changed. She was changed to something shivering, wide and reaching. She wanted to cover her face, but she could not. She trembled to know the calling would pierce her, magenta welling in her soul. His fingers seared where she felt him.

"I think some part of that woman's body is with you still," Addison said. "Do you not feel it so?"

Emmy's hard, cold fear ran down the walls as bright water.

"I want Daddy to come home," she said, and felt the terrible truth fall into her stomach. "I want to go home." The voices whispered an endless, forever winter. They were tongues like dead leaves, and the wind moved them in a great abyss of quiet and nothingness. They would never be done with her. She knew it now. She believed him.

On the night the power went off in Beulah Creek, the town was farther away than ever from Millsborough and the lowlands. Children went to bed crying for their mothers or fathers, wishing the long mountain roads would carry them home at last. Other folks drew up thick, warm covers against the wintry dark and did not get up until they could see the next morning. They felt calamity coming for them and were afraid. They closed their eyes to make the dark go away. Only one light burned in the town. Out in his workshop, Noah Carpenter was laboring by lamplight. He did not feel the cold until dawn.

IV

The serving platter slipped from Malathy Joan's fingers and shattered across her kitchen floor in a fine, violent rain. She blinked at the bitter sound of breaking and then stood and looked at the cream-colored shards. It had been long since she had dropped a fragile thing. She did not know how she had done it.

Breathing evenly, she went to the closet and took out the broom and dustpan with fingers as firm and steady as she could place them in those days. She swept up the pieces, placing her bare feet carefully upon the wooden floor. It did not matter that things now went to pieces in her hands. She still would turn her hands to the work that she knew. If her hands were not idle, the dark questions could not drop into them like clusters of berries and their thorns. She tossed the bits of platter into the trash, twisting her wrist to let them fall.

High on Sumac Hill, the sun fell in bold, golden beams. Addison had stood from the breakfast table and gone to enjoy the day, and Emmy had lifted her young eyes to his face and followed. Where before the girl had slunk sidelong from his sight, she followed him now as though he tapped his thigh and whistled to bid her come. Malathy Joan did not accompany them. She glanced from the kitchen window at the shining trees above the house. Their loveliness saddened her, and she turned away. She wished the snows would shrivel to water so that Clement Foster could come at last to reclaim his daughter, for she wearied of sharing her home and her guest with the girl.

Malathy Joan placed a bowl of table scraps on the floor for Pumpkin and stroked the long, lean line of his back when he came to eat. She carried clean plates to the cupboard and shut the door upon them. Her fingers trailed briefly upon the wood. In the place behind her ribs where she had known Noah, had known without question that he would come to her, there was nothing now but gaping dark and the blood of her life. She took off her apron and hung it on its peg.

For the first time since she had come to live in the Greenberry house, Malathy Joan walked through rooms that closed about her, hot and dim. She reached and tugged the covers where she made Emmy's bed on the couch, but wrinkles would return before she passed by again. Each day she took up a dust cloth and wiped the mantelpiece clean, and each day white powder lay thick on dresser top and table as though months had slipped through the house while she slept. She pressed her hand to her forehead and whispered the spirit's name, knowing.

"Are you glad to give me trouble?" she said. "Or else what can you mean to tell me?"

The smell of lilacs filled her mouth and throat. She rose later and later in the mornings, and sometimes, in the midst of cutting roses or drying dishes, she felt a sliver of hollowness in her chest like a hairline crack in a china cup. Her fingers would stray to her collarbone but grasped only the fabric of her blouse. There was no longer any silver to touch, and after much searching in the crevices of the house, she slowly lost its feel. She wondered if this, too, were Jess's wish to give her, as the mountains began to cast their dark, rock faces across her soul.

Beulah Creek had its share of dark places that morning. When Grandma Barnes stepped into her own kitchen, the air crackled cold about the old woman's bare shins. She knew what it was that Malathy Joan had taken into the Greenberry house, and the knowing weighed on her bones like coming rain.

In the dim light of snowfall, she tugged open a cabinet door and reached down a can of pears for breakfast, since neither she nor anyone else in the town had power still. She did not know that high on Sumac Hill, among the graves, Addison had presented Emmy Foster dead words on dead rock, but the old woman would not have wondered had she learned of it. Lucien Brown had long ago taught disquieting things to the young Hazel Barnes as he sat in the grass, one knee drawn up toward his chest and one arm spread across the knee as though he were broad and open, generous with her. He had told her once that some folks could watch the grass grow and figure how high it would stand, but the power lay in the hand that mowed it down.

Grandma Barnes pulled open a drawer for the can opener. She fitted it to the lid and twisted the knob so that the opener bit into the lid and began its slow, gnawing crawl around the top. She remembered plenty about the summer Lucien Brown spent among them. As in other summers, she had let June bugs creep into her hands so she could see their green glazed scales. She had lain motionless at the edge of the creek to watch the puff of a frog's throat or the head of a turtle peer out at the world with its old eyes. She had been her mother's daughter and so could go where she would, unchecked. She had scowled back at any face that frowned her way.

One afternoon late in that summer, full of the lazy, honeyed hum of insects, Hazel Barnes had rested on her stomach in the grass by the creek, slowly waving her bare feet back and forth through the September sunlight. She had watched an ugly, black beetle as it struggled through the stalks. Its legs had jerked and flailed as its small body rocked its funny dance to wherever it would go. Pants legs had approached her, then, through the grass to sit on the large, flat stone nearby. His shape cast across the ground. She did not bother to look. She folded her hands beneath her knobby chin. She could hold her wonder cupped like a lightning bug, and she could release it again as she chose. She chose to keep it just then. She enjoyed the beetle.

"Pretty day, isn't it, Hazel?" Lucien had said to her.

She watched the shiny insect sway along busily, unknowing. Lucien abruptly raised his foot and dropped it where the beetle went. She blinked at his quickness and the snap of the grass. But the beetle still lived. It rocked backwards and squirmed its legs. Lucien laughed a slow, soft laugh.

Hazel flicked her eyes to him then. It was the same head she expected, ringed with yellow curls, the lips like a woman's. It looked pretty and then some. He was watching her sidelong.

"My schoolmaster taught me of insects," he said. "Are they not curious, these creeping things?"

She looked back to the beetle. It turned its body and began scrambling through the grass once more, tracing the length of Lucien's foot.

"It has no notion what's happened to it," he said. "But you and I do, Hazel. And there's power in that."

The ugly beetle rounded the toe of Lucien's shoe. Its legs wriggled across the grass stalks as it went on its way. It seemed clumsy and weak. She thought she knew what Lucien meant, that the days grew sharp and short, and one day soon, the hum of wings would be stilled.

"There's power in knowing," he said. "Not everyone can see so clearly, the way you can do."

She eyed him again, her mouth pinched closed. He followed her sometimes and brought words to give her. She knew no other grown man like him. She liked to hear his mind spread out like clothes on a line. Most grown people talked behind their hands. She did not fear the gentle way he used his lips to make such cold words.

"What things do you know?" he asked her. "Do you never tell anyone, Hazel?"

She lifted herself from the ground and sat back on her heels. "I know enough," she said.

He was a creature as curious as any, wild and cunning for all his well-turned words. She had watched him creep more than once from the back of the Greenberry house and figured one did not have to see very far to see what was right before them. The pattern of birds across the heavens or the hot, smoky look of a guilty man's face told her what was coming, death or winter. It was all a soul needed to know.

Grandma Barnes took up a spoon and scooped the canned pears into a clean bowl. This morning, she would stand by the kitchen window and eat her pears and watch the snow cover the earth. The dog would come clicking into the room and eat its food. She knew these things would happen, so she would stand and eat until the visitor came. She figured one would come. She reckoned she had a fair notion what would be asked of her that morning.

So when Grandma Barnes spied Noah Carpenter trudging through the cold and the pale wet to her back doorstep, looking morose and worn down and crumpled like he'd been sitting in corners all night instead of sleeping, she set down her pears and went to open the door. The dog at its food bowl lifted its head and made a low, whimpering sound.

"Hush," she told it. "Just letting in a little more trouble this morning, is all. Don't have enough to do me."

She jerked open the door before Noah knocked. The world was still dreaming in purple and soft yellow, but the face before her was hard and dark and real. She made a curt movement with her hand and pushed the head of her cane towards him.

"No good mornings here today," she said. "That's not why you dragged over here, Noah Carpenter, and it scarce seven o'clock."

Noah stood and regarded her. His eyes glittered. Slowly, thoughtfully, he took off his hat and looked at it there in his hand. She waited. There was no telling what Noah was ever going to say, only that he was going to ponder it awhile first, and it was going to be thorough and pretty well powerful when he got around to saying it.

"I reckon you recollect when Jess Greenberry died," he said, at last.

She stiffened her fingers about her cane. "I recollect when," she said. "Jess died in 19 and 19." She recalled a great block of ice wedged in her own chest, cold enough to hurt, and the tall backs of grown men and women. She remembered the woman's hands clasped upon the motionless abdomen, the waxen face melted in strange lines, the same way she remembered the lifeless creatures pierced through by pins in Lucien's cigar box. She had seen the power of knowing, and it was desolation.

Noah lifted his head. His grim, black eyes looked at her steadily. "I figured maybe there was something I ought to know."

Grandma Barnes grunted. "You already know what you ought, Noah Carpenter. There's nothing to know besides."

He stood and said nothing. Over his shoulder, the world was brightening. Still he stood. He had set his mouth tight and fearsome as though it would never move again. She remembered the solemn child at his grandpa's side, listening, watching, while grown folks talked on. Always Noah had waited, touching nothing and no one.

She stepped back. "Well, get in here, then."

He nodded. "Yes, ma'am." He kicked the snow off his boots and came into the kitchen. As Noah took off his jacket, she saw there was sawdust on his shirtsleeves. She had never known Noah to be anything but clean when he came calling.

"I'm just finishing my pears," she said, walking away from him. "You're welcome to what there is." She took up the bowl.

"I don't care for anything just now," he said. His boots took him through the doorway into her front room. "Thank you anyhow."

She ate the rest of her breakfast, watching the day come into her yard. She listened for Noah in the next room, but he was quiet. He knew when to let things be, most times. Then she rinsed the bowl and placed it in the sink. As she walked into the front room, Noah stood with his back to her. He was looking long and hard at the faded print of the Last Supper, slightly crooked on the wall near the coal stove. She paused on her way and waited.

Deliberately, like he answered what no one asked, he said, "I don't like what I'm seeing up there." He didn't move, just stood with his hands clasped behind him. "Things aren't right somehow."

His back was a rock to break bones upon. She went over to her old green armchair. "They'll never be right, till the Lord comes again. What was done, is done, and will be again, if she chooses to keep her home with the devil and with dead things." She sat with great care. "What do you want me to do?"

He pondered the stove. Then, real quiet, he said, "I won't let this be." He turned. For all his soft, well-mannered talk, there were sharp things in his eyes, no matter what he was saying. "What went with Jess Greenberry might be good to know."

She sighed so thoroughly her chest hurt. "There's a chair here if you'd like to sit," she said, and moved her hand. The dog whimpered from the kitchen.

"Yes, ma'am, I believe I will." Noah came to the plain, ladder-back chair and sat, filling it as though he were made of the same wood, a good fit. Then the house was still. Warmth curled about them from the stove. Outside, the sun was taken up into the clouds, and the snow trailed as crumbs of heaven upon the earth.

"This is what I was told once," said Grandma Barnes, and thought of Lucien. "A friend of mine said that the ones that knew things must never tell them, because folks wouldn't understand, and ruin would come regardless. Well, I've told and seen ruin come, and I've kept quiet and seen it come the same."

Noah nodded, a single, solemn movement.

"When they buried Jess Greenberry," she said, "I heard what was said. Grown folks wouldn't speak dark things in front of a child, but I knew how to come and go so they wouldn't see. They said Jess would have had herself another baby, if she had lived." The skin twitched at the corner of her lips. "Some said that what Jess was carrying wasn't Saul's. Some said none of them babies was his. I don't know the truth of that. I know they cut Jess Greenberry down from the rafters in that house, and only the good Lord knows who strung her up there."

Noah's face was as stern as the timbers of a barn raw and weathered in a stony field. He looked nothing like Saul Greenberry, did not have the high forehead or the bristling beard of a patriarch, but Grandma Barnes discerned the brooding spirits of both men.

"This is how it was," said Grandma Barnes. "Jess was an Evans girl, and she and Opal, her sister, married Greenberry brothers. Opal was round and sweet and lovely, and Ezra was good to her, brought her candy and pretty things. Those were the Greenberrys who stayed in Beulah Creek."

"Ruth Foster's people," said Noah. Something shifted in his eyes.

"Yes. You can see it in Emmy. Opal's milky face," said Grandma Barnes. "Not like Jess." She squinted, remembering the red-haired Evans sisters. "There's been no one like Jess in Beulah Creek these many years."

Jess would come shining into a room, tall and hale, rosy and laughing. Grandma Barnes had a clear thought of her in a knot of young ladies on a Sunday afternoon. Jess tipped back her head and laughed, her teeth bright, her eyes keen with pleasure. It was a strong laugh that made faces turn towards her. Hazel had known even then that Jess turned her eye to see who watched and laughed all the merrier when she caught faces peering. Nobody who saw that vibrant sight would have guessed how soon the woman's death would come. Grandma Barnes shifted in the armchair, feeling a strain.

"Now all that's left is Jess's spirit in that house up the hill," she said, "festering. Saul didn't stay. He took those three babies and left out of here the day after they laid Jess Greenberry in the ground. Nobody knows any more of them."

Noah was looking at his hands folded together like a crumpled prayer. He did not speak.

"It was an astonishment to us all when Jess married Saul. Jess was pert and nineteen, and Saul was as stern and humorless a man as ever lived," said Grandma Barnes. "He farmed his land and traveled all through these mountains, preaching where the Lord led him. He seemed a good man, one who worked where he went. And I reckon he loved her. The day they cut her down, they found him wandering about the creek bottom like a night shadow. He said he had found her so, and then he never said another word in Beulah Creek."

Grandma Barnes grew quiet then. She looked at the thin curtains drawn across the window, holding the light of snow. "Jess didn't laugh near so often after the babies started coming. The first followed pretty quick after she married, and then she couldn't travel with Saul when he went preaching. She was used to doing as she liked, making folks look at her. But after she married, she kept to herself, kept to that house."

In the quiet left by Grandma Barnes's words, the year died all around them, slowly.

"And then they found her." Noah spoke to his hands.

"Or Saul did, if you believe that," said Grandma Barnes. "Yes. There were those who wondered why it came about. But I knew." She drew breath, for she had not spoken the name in all the years since. "There was Lucien Brown." She had dared to tell Jess what became of him, had dared because Hazel knew what the sneaking from the back door had meant, and because she, too, had lost Lucien because of it. By that next evening Jess Greenberry was dead. That was a weighty thing to carry.

"Lucien was one of Saul's lost souls," Grandma Barnes told Noah, "one gleaned too early." She had watched at her mother's side as Saul brought the tall, lithe, blue-eyed man into their midst. She had heard the words said of the stranger. He came from a far place and was a learned, musical man who met with Saul at a camp meeting. His face was fair and careful, empty of pride. But she had watched his eyes taking greedy looks when he thought no one saw. "We moved at the edge of things in Beulah Creek," said Grandma Barnes, "the both of us. My daddy was dead, and Lucien was a stranger man. He was the devil's own son, but he was a powerful friend to me all the same."

Her face grew very still. "Nobody thought to ask whatever went with him until Jess was buried and Saul long gone from here. Even then they didn't wonder overmuch."

"What went with him?" said Noah in a low voice.

Her eyes narrowed, and she shook her head. She was not going to speak of it.

"That boy up there puts me awful much in mind of him, if you want to know." She stood with the help of her cane. "And I reckon I've seen plenty and said enough." The rest was hers, stark and naked and dead as the insects in Lucien's cigar box, pinned in the semblance of life forever. Not even the carpenter would get it out of her in this world.

Noah kept studying his hands in his lap. She wondered what he was aiming to do with them.

"You want to know what will be, I can't tell you that," she said. "All I know is that anyone who ever came in the shadow of that house has kept that shadow across their soul all their days."

Grandma Barnes watched Noah, who stayed quiet for a time. Then he unclasped his hands and got to his feet. He paused there, looking at the pale, sheer curtains. His face was as silent as ever, but she watched his fingers twitch as he gripped them at his sides. It was an unsettling thing to see. Grandma Barnes had known honest hands to wander before to danger.

"Your knees still work, don't they?" she asked.

He nodded. "Reckon they do yet." He sounded worn down and unpleasant.

"Well, use them for what God intended." She did not like to let Abel's grandson go off with his hands unsteady. He lived by his hands, and they were strong. Unquiet, they could slip, they could break things as he gripped the shaft of a hammer, the bones of a neck.

Noah nodded again, hesitantly, as though he were answering something altogether different. "I'd best get along home," he said at last. "Thank you for the trouble." Only then did he face her. There was an ugly tightness in his brow, and neither thanks nor welcome in his eyes. She could tell that was not all he had to say. But he walked into the kitchen anyway and took up his hat and wool jacket.

The dog cried out. Grandma Barnes felt the strangeness of her body, halting and shriveled, that could not cross the floor as she would. But if she could, he would not stop. He was like his mama, Abilene, in that way.

"You watch yourself, now," she called after him.

The door closed softly, but Grandma Barnes could not get the sound out of her head the rest of the day. She wrapped in quilts by the coal stove and heard it in the light breath of snow upon the world. She heard it in the unquiet sleep of the dog. She heard it as she closed her eyes. It was the sound of the cigar box tapping shut upon insect corpses. Lucien Brown had pinned them there to admire them, and his eyes laughed over them.

That next twilight afternoon in Beulah Creek, Jack Hendrick, too, received company, which surprised him. Jack had tired of sitting in the house in the dark while Judy talked on the phone to her sister in Virginia. So he went and sat in the dark by himself in the store. He looked at the empty shelves. He listened to the radio while the batteries slowly ran down. He read the same two-week-old newspaper he had read the day before. The clock on the wall had stopped when the power went off, at a few minutes after six o'clock.

So he did not know how long he had been sitting there when the bells on the door rang. Half-hearing the sound, he turned, but his eyes knew what they were seeing at once.

Malathy Joan came through the door with her long, black shawl wrapped over her head. Her bare fingers curved about the handle of the basket she carried. Her brown skirts were wet from the snow. With one hand, she reached up and drew the shawl down from around her head. Her hair glistened where the snowflakes had fallen, and her eyes looked like they belonged to one of the wild, fleet-footed, prairie creatures from a foreign land, the ones with horns as delicate as church spires. Jack couldn't remember the names of any just then, but he knew they were like names out of the Bible, nearly too fantastic to be true. She looked about the store as though she were not quite sure how she had come there.

He must have gotten down from the stool. "Afternoon," he said, which seemed a pitiful thing to say. He was still clutching the newspaper, so he began folding it up. "Haven't seen you down here in a long while."

"Yes," said Malathy Joan, in her hoarse, husky voice. Her eyes finally found his face, and he stopped moving, the newspaper half folded in his hands. He dimly realized that this was foolish. She would not leap away into the winter forest if he moved too suddenly.

"Would you take these?" she asked. She held out the basket, which was covered with an embroidered cloth and seemed heavy. "Please, give them to anyone who needs them."

Jack dumped the newspaper onto the counter. "Well . . . I reckon I can do that. What have you got there?"

"A beginning," she said. "I can bring more another day. I have many jars like these." She did not come any nearer, only stood and offered the basket. "I know it is cold, down here."

He felt a slow frown deepen in his chest. There were plenty of other folks she could have come to see, bringing baskets and her plain, sad face and whatever else she thought to bestow. He knew of one carpenter who would not have been sorry of a sight of her.

"That's right nice of you," said Jack. He managed to get himself around the counter. "Emmy doing all right with you?" He considered where he could put his hands to take the basket. She had such long fingers.

"I believe Emmy's well, if a little homesick. She didn't want to come down here today," said Malathy Joan. "She wanted to stay with her cat."

It was at that moment Jack glimpsed the figure on the other side of the door. He was horrified to think it was Judy, bringing him a supper or a scarf. He was even more astonished to see that it was a man, young-looking and a stranger. He could not think how anyone had traveled to Beulah Creek in the hard crush of winter. The man wore no coat.

"Come on in here," said Jack, motioning with his arm. Malathy Joan turned her head to see where he looked.

In answer, the young man took the door handle with his left hand, and Jack saw then that he carried a second basket, covered also with a cloth. A cold sharpness came to Jack's throat. This was no stranger to Malathy Joan. Hardly more than a boy walked cautiously, carefully into the store. He had a hitch to his step. His face was like a dishrag and his long hair like rusty water. He seemed poor and scrawny to Jack, and there was a pinched, narrow look to his eye.

"You been in town long?" Jack said.

The boy shook his head. Lips peeled back from straight, white teeth. "But I like it here, though."

Malathy Joan placed her long face once more before Jack's widening eyes. "This is Addison," she said to Jack. "He's been at my house and unwell, but he's nearly mended now. He came this morning to help bring the food. He's often been a help to me. This is Jack Hendrick, Addison," she said, peering over her shoulder. Her hair smelled rich and purple.

Jack tried to watch what was happening. He felt guilty to watch it.

Addison nodded. "I've heard the name before." The young man's voice was as smooth and sparkling as ice. "You're the man that feeds this little town." A quirk pulled at the edge of the lips.

Jack wondered what this boy wanted with him and with her. Jack gripped the basket away from Malathy Joan with rawness in his throat and could hardly bear to see her. Her face was a hall of empty trees. Her bones were sharp and delicate as frost. He had always wanted to know someplace like she was. He wanted to tell her not to go. The room around them billowed into wisps of grey. He wanted to tell her to go and never return. Beulah Creek was no place for her.

Addison walked forward and placed the basket he carried on the counter. The jars clanked and rattled.

"We should go now," said Malathy Joan. Her fingers moved to her collarbone. She closed them upon nothing. "Thank you, Jack," she said. She turned toward Addison. Her hair moved like the fall of night upon the high ridges, coming down into secret places of rock and snow.

"Thank you," said Jack after them. Malathy Joan and Addison went to the door and then out into the coming year, which yawned cold at him before the door closed again. He felt long stretches of winter inside him and did not know what it meant. He tried to think what words he could tell Noah Carpenter. There were none he wanted to give.

Neither did Noah Carpenter like the feel of the dim, chill air as it clutched for him. Stepping carefully from the back step of his house, he labored through the snow to his workshop. His breath caught in the raw, sore places. It was not that he had ceased to have faith in Malathy Joan. It was that he had no answer to give her. The ones that came to him troubled him more than anything he had seen up at the Greenberry house.

He blinked against fine, tiny bits of snow as he walked and thought. He should not go to her. It was not in him to go. She was of one mind about that boy. He allowed as much, and he would leave her to it. He was of another altogether. He tried not to think what might happen if the ice got down into him and busted him apart. He was feeling himself a long way from thawing.

Once inside the cold shed, he looked again, in daylight, at the thing his hands had made. He cupped his fingers to his mouth and breathed on them. He had gone into his workshop in the night not knowing what he was making. But his hands would not be still, and his dreams were enough to wake him. When he had closed his eyes, he had seen only smears of pale hair and dark blood. There was nothing for him to do but bring a lantern and turn his hands to something useful.

As he worked, the thing beneath his fingers had taken shape and become a candlestick. He went over now and moved his thumb upon the curve of the dark wood. It felt familiar, steadying, to follow the smoothness as it rounded beneath his touch. He figured it satisfied him, though he had to admit it didn't give him much ease in the end. She was a woman to do things for, and this was all he knew.

He took the candlestick and carried it into the house. He placed it where he thought best, on the table in the center of the living room. There it would stay until something better came to him. He reckoned he meant it for her.

The new year stole into Beulah Creek with twisted, empty arms. It reached down and covered the windows with its cold hand as it passed. People saw the glass streaked pale and ugly and knew despair. In the night, Veeny Anderson searched for the bookmark that had laid in her Bible for forty years. She got dutifully down on her knees and peered under every piece of furniture in her house, wielding a flashlight and pressing a hand to her heart. It was smothering work, but all she found was a nickel and some crumbs of bread. Her brother had sent the bookmark to her from a foreign land that wove fabric in astonishing hues. It was hard to know she had lost the gift of her only brother, dead all those years ago and buried in a land where his people had never been.

One evening, Betty McGuire, carrying a cold supper to Anson Bledsoe, glanced at the old man's house as she passed the hydrangea bushes and cried out in unbelief. The cellar doors had been forced, and Mason jars of beans and tomatoes were cracked open and bleeding in the snow. Sarah Mullins was horrified one morning to walk into her daughters' bedroom to find the window standing wide. The girls could remember nothing but a dream about an angel, a boy angel, they both insisted, who had come and sat upon their bed and knew everything about them, like songs and ice cream and horses they liked best. Melinda wanted the palomino, but Miranda desired nothing but the sleek black horse with the soft nose. It had eaten sugar right out of her hand, she said. The girls went about that day with sad eyes and weepy voices, and that night, they slept in the bed with Sarah.

The people of Beulah Creek were weary and grieved, waiting for folks to return from the lowlands and the snow to melt away. In the end, most took cold lies to bed and pressed against them in the dark, among the handmade quilts, seeking comfort where there was none. Even Noah Carpenter, who would not look January in the face, paused as he closed the shutters. His eyes strayed up the high slope to where the Greenberry house stood. There was no candlestick ever made that could keep off the dark on its own. It was like splinters in the tenderest parts of his hand, burrowing into the skin and festering, to consider what was being done to her. Neither was it at all comfortable to think on what he himself might do.

V

The Greenberry house was not visited by January like any other place in Beulah Creek. The nights there were strong with an odor like wet, hot leaves decaying into loam. Malathy Joan breathed it as she lay wrapped in a patchwork quilt on the hardwood floor. No matter how she turned, she could not find rest. Her long braid pressed into her spine. She shivered with the cold of icicles inside her bones. Then the floor was hot, and she stretched upon a grate over coals that burned blue and orange. She fingered the stitching on the quilt where it was coming free and ached in every place she had ever known.

At last, she got to her feet, unfolding her long body slowly, the quilt held about her to keep its weight close. Hoping not to wake Emmy who slept on the couch, she slipped to the front door.

The stars above her showed her what she had come to find. She walked to the edge of the porch and then carefully down the steps to the grass rich within the indigo dark. Through the garden she walked towards the slope of the hill. Sometimes she could smell the vegetables and flowers, black and bubbling, but mostly she smelled steaming midnight dripping through the air.

She paused as she neared the slope overlooking the town. The empty place upon her chest was tender, as though rubbed too long by wind and water and unkind fabric. With both hands grasping the ends of quilt at her throat, she looked down on the banks of Beulah Creek, at the end of one road and the beginning of another. She did not know where the other road led, beyond the mountains. She could barely see the houses beneath her feet.

"Jess," she whispered. "Is this what you saw?"

Malathy heard the rustle of the grass only when it stopped close by. She did not turn around. She was not afraid of what was there.

"What is it that you see?" Addison asked. "Isn't it late to be out here?"

She shook her head. "I came to look at things." She still sought the contours of the creek bottom in among the shadows.

"They have not welcomed you," he said.

She lifted her head towards the dark, wild hills. Her fingers ached to trace the pattern of her talisman, to know herself at peace.

"I was called, but not for this," she said. "I did not come here for this." Her arms drew the quilt tight across her chest. "I am neighbor to almost no one here."

Addison walked very near. She heard the grass hiss.

"I think it was wrong of your friend to leave you the way he did," he said, his words low. "If you must know."

She smelled the stink of the garden, blighted from too much sun. "Please don't speak against him," she whispered. The words cut the flesh of her throat. She remembered again how Noah had turned from her, and the remembrance echoed in the ghostly rooms of her soul, beneath the place her silver pendant had hung. She had had many hopes of her good friend once.

"Maybe I could learn to feel as you do," said Addison, "to believe in something if it doesn't seem to believe in you. I don't know. It seems a hard choice to me."

He touched the hair about her face. She felt him, and she shivered.

"It's the choice I must make," she said. "I am lost here otherwise."

Addison's hand was flesh and blood, and though she could not see it for the dark, she knew it was as beautiful as anything she could wish. She found that she wanted him there, could even need him. They could be friends to one another in a mountain town that did not want to know them. The night lay heavy over the tops of trees and ridges, pressed upon the settlement below, and kept both of them close.

In time, at last, the snow clouds cleared from Beulah Creek, and the sun returned. Buildings glittered along the water as tin roofs of barns, of sheds, of houses, caught the winter sun like some brilliant sorcery. Jack Hendrick started awake at the hum of freezer cases, while back home, Judy snapped on the television and knelt before it, amazed with gratitude. As snow shriveled from steps and from driveways, people turned their ears to hear the sound of water. They rejoiced to hear it, for the road that wound so graciously, so benevolently from the lowlands could begin to carry their loved ones back to them.

When Clement Foster came to the Greenberry house finally for his daughter, Malathy fetched her from the woods of Sumac Hill. At first, the girl blinked at her father as though he had grown too bright for her. Then she broke free of Malathy's hand and ran to catch hold of him. Emmy grasped his shirt and pressed her face against it. Clement held and patted the child. Malathy Joan watched the two of them embracing in the sunlight. She felt she had neglected Emmy in ways she regretted but had found herself unable to help. Emmy had become skittish and strange, speaking seldom to her where before the girl had been so free. Malathy did not understand how Addison's presence seemed to alter the affections of those around her. She was troubled, too, by turnings that had taken place inside herself and wondered what he wanted there in Beulah Creek, if he would go or stay, and why.

Addison had already gone into the town to walk about. After Clement and Emmy set off down the hill home, Malathy Joan sat in the rocking chair in the front room of the Greenberry house. She listened to the creak of the wood as she eased the chair to and fro. She smelled the old wood of the house and her new, braided rugs and the dark given off from the walls. Somewhere a bird chirped. Its song came once, twice, four times, and then no more. Still she rocked. She left the clean clothing in its basket, rumpled. The gathering of it into her lap, the smoothing of it into crisp corners, seemed more than her arms could hold just then. If the ghost woman were to walk from the wall, she would give her words full. Perhaps they could grieve together the lives they had lost.

She heard a sudden clatter from the kitchen. She stopped at once the squeak and moan of the chair. She tightened her grip on the arms, her back hardened into certainty. She rose, hardly thinking what she went to do. She crossed the few steps to the kitchen to see what had happened. Her heartbeat told her that she would find Jess Greenberry beyond the doorway.

She reached the threshold and stopped. She gripped the door facing.

Jess lay sprawled on her side on the floor, a hand raised to her cheek. A kitchen chair had toppled beside her. Her face was closed and tightened in a deep grief that came in bursts of silence from her mouth. Long strands of strawberry hair trailed loose down her shoulders. Her body jerked and shook. Watching, Malathy Joan felt a terrible fullness in her chest that crushed about her heart and lungs. Someone stood behind Jess, a large blurred form that was surely Saul, tall and broad-shouldered. His arm was lifted and drawn across his body. It seemed that he was speaking to Jess, for something was moving where his face would be.

Then he reached down and grabbed the woman's arm. Malathy Joan heard herself cry out. In the same moment, Jess's eyes flew open. They showed forth a chilling light, utterly distant from the violence Jess suffered there, long ago.

Saul pulled Jess to her feet, her body stiffening as she left the floor. Malathy Joan threw herself across the space between the lost woman and her. In that moment, she apprehended the woman's coming death, though she did not know when it had come or how. She saw, too, the sharp pieces of her own life. She held out her hands to tear Jess Greenberry away. She would take this upon her. The house would rest. The captive soul would be released. Her act took no thought, but was her belief moving through her long bones and sinews. She believed her arms so strong.

Malathy Joan's hands found the fabric of the woman's sleeve, and the figure of Saul melted away. She touched a cold that froze the breath to the roof of her mouth. She had meant to speak but could not. Jess turned her face near, and the room dwindled into the spirit woman's eyes.

Malathy Joan had no power to open her hands. She clutched a pale vapor that seeped into her skin. Her insides crawled with fire as though she were diseased. In her soul moved other shapes, the image of a woman slowly rocking before the window, a woman whose heart shriveled from the midwife's daughter's words, whose mind filled with jagged rocks and slivers of metal. The one she loved would come no more. The one she loved lay dead. Her husband had confirmed it at supper, his hands steady as he lifted his fork to his mouth. There had been weeping and shouting then, and blows and threats of worse, but the end would not lie there.

Looking at Jess, Malathy Joan felt the writhing of serpents, digging within her a hollowness without bottom. Mountains clutched such seas beneath their roots, where no living soul had dived to the depths or sailed to the far shore. She saw love scattered on the waters, gleaming like red gold, but ripples pulled and stretched it into lurid tatters. Permeable as she had not been in so very long, she stood and looked into Jess Greenberry until she knew her. The knowing turned her blood slow and dark.

After the passing of many hours, when at last she opened her eyes, she saw that she stood alone.

"Malathy?" Addison called from outside. "Malathy Joan?"

His voice came to her from the front of the house. She drifted slowly through the darkening rooms until she reached the porch. Outside, she narrowed her eyes against the setting of the sun. Addison sat with his feet on the stone step, his back to her. As she came closer, he looked at her over his shoulder.

"It's getting dark," he said. He turned his body, leaning against one of the posts that held the roof over them. "Don't you think it's beautiful to watch it come? A gentle thing, like a hand come down to touch the earth."

She walked to the edge of the porch and lifted her eyes. The sky was going up in flames. Among the burned-out remnants, tiny embers glowed gold and scarlet. The sight of it touched her in strange ways. She was not entirely herself.

"Yes," she said, "yes, it is beautiful, and it is terrible also. It is hard to see in the dark, hard to know where to put your foot or your hand. It is hard for people to find one another in the dark."

"I've met many in the dark," said Addison. He was looking at her through the reddening light, around the post. "I think people huddle together and help one another when they walk through it, letting it fall against them as it will."

She put her fingers around the post. "I wished for rootedness," she said. "I wanted that here, in this house, in this small town in the mountains where I believed I should be." She shook her head. "And yet it has taken every beat of my heart, all the blood that runs through me, to hold this house over my head."

Addison leaned towards her and put his hand on the post between them. "You could let it go," he said.

"I do not know where I would be then." The garden roiled black and purple before her, reeking. She looked down at the boards beneath her feet.

"You'd be free to go where you would. There's the world to house you."

She felt herself wavering, incorporeal, ethereal, like the flame of a candle nearly gone. "How will I gather the world?" She closed her eyes and pressed her forehead to the post. "How will I light it? How will I sweep and tend it?" Her fingers cramped. "I am not afraid," she said. "But the cold, sad weight of it will break every bone in me."

She heard the rustle of clothing, then, heard Addison's feet press against the old boards. She could feel him standing by her, with only the post between them.

"This is what I know," he said. "The world doesn't believe in me or in you either. It goes on the way it goes, and I've learned to let it. That's not kind of me, perhaps." His words seemed hard, and yet when he spoke them, they drifted over her to settle like dusk upon the mountains. "Your heart is large, Malathy Joan, if you would take the whole world into it for safekeeping."

She was too dry even to weep. "You cannot speak of my heart," she rasped. "It is not at all as you think it."

"You can tell me how I am to think of it, then," he said.

When Malathy Joan's head came up, and her eyes were opened, she reached where Addison had placed his hand. It was warm and firm, the flesh slightly yielding where she touched it. He did not tense or move from her. She gathered up his hand in hers and took it from the post.

"I cannot hold the pieces together anymore," she said. "I cannot hold them at all."

She did not plead with him, but only said what she knew to be true. She laid his palm upon her breast above the living heart beneath. He cupped his hand beneath hers. She heard him breathing, and she breathed also.

"You trust me to hold the pieces for you," he said. It was and was not a question. He brought his head very close to her. His hair smelled of grass on a summer hill, ripening toward autumn, golden, dusty, a little smoky.

"We can give help to each other," she said. She raised her long, thin fingers and spread them against the side of his face, resting them lightly there. "I do not like to think of you broken and lost."

He placed his hands into the small of her back so that she was encircled by his bones, so that she could go nowhere that he was not. "Then you are thinking of me," he said.

She felt a twinge in her spine, a chill not unpleasant. She trailed her thumb upon the skin of his face and knew what she touched was beautiful. His jaw tightened. In the dark of late January, among the indigo, the violet shadows, she found that she was thinking of him, and she did not know when it had begun.

"Yes," she whispered.

She stretched out her head upon her neck and put her lips to his. He kissed her in return. His hands gripped her until she could no longer feel her legs to move them. Her bones had turned to water.

From that night, Malathy Joan no longer laid down upon the couch to sleep. She went to her bed covered in the white chenille bedspread and took Addison with her. She hungered where she had once been full. She held out her arms where once she had kept them close to her body. The wandering spirit had entered the marrow of her bones and left her changed.

Sometimes she had a sharpening of vision that pierced her eyes until they hurt, and thoughts seized her that she could not call her own. She awakened late in the mornings naked, the bedclothes tangled about her long, dark limbs. Sometimes Addison would lie beside her when she woke, and she touched him to know she lived. Sometimes she woke and heard him in the kitchen, the smell of coffee rising up to the rafters. She lay back on the pillow and let herself hover between waking and dreaming, between believing and doubting. She folded her hands together and let her thoughts wander, until she thought she had come to Beulah Creek for no other reason than to share her emptiness with another vagrant soul.

Still once in the night as Addison made love to her, and the weight and warmth and thrust of his body made each nerve keen, so that every pore of her stood open, and her eyes were wide, Malathy Joan watched as Jess stood beside the bed. Around the spirit woman's neck hung a string of pearls, and the woman caressed the pearls and smiled at her. An icy blackness swept into her heart as Malathy remembered the silver circle once on her own hale, strong breastbone. The thought fell from her mind as quickly as she had found it, though, and it drowned in the haze of lilacs that washed into her.

The town of Beulah Creek spread itself along the creek banks all unknowing. Those who lived there kept doors and windows locked, kept themselves to the far corners of their houses and crouched away from one another. If a wife looked at her husband, if a brother caught his brother in the way, ugly words oozed from mouths like running sores. Cakes fell, and bread burned. The canned foods that the stranger woman had brought to Jack's store and that people had greedily snatched from the shelves were now pitched into the trash. The taste turned in people's mouths and sickened their stomachs.

When the winter wind blew with its paring edge, the Beulah Creek dwellers seemed to lose pieces of themselves, the tip of a finger or of a nose, perhaps. Bright cold seeped into the cuts until hardly a soul in the settlement did not feel raw and wounded. They turned their eyes to the Greenberry house and cursed the ground it stood upon without knowing why. Neither did Malathy Joan know anything that befell her neighbors in the town. Through the nights when January and then February shone upon the landscape chill and clear and white, she lay in the arms of the beautiful young man with the melodious voice and lived her days as though all her seeking were done.

VI

It was not long before those who returned to Beulah Creek suspected that winter had bowed a few backs too low, twisting and maiming, just as it had broken limbs from trees in backyards. Clement Foster, for one, was at a loss to know what the matter of the snow had been. His daughter had gone silent, her face crushed like pale silk, like the face of a long, slow illness.

After he brought her down from the Greenberry house, she took to sitting in the old green recliner in the corner of the living room and looking out the front window, her grey eyes stillborn. If the curtains were drawn, she watched the curtains. Pumpkin would come and stand at her feet and mew, and she would reach down and touch his head as though, with regret, she knew she could give him no more.

Clement believed his daughter was weary of the snow and the sameness, that she had grown sad at being gone from home. From the time she was a baby, he had never left her so long. Their first night back, he had opened a can of the little spaghetti circles she used to love. He heated the food on the stove and carried it to her. As he approached her with the warm plate and a glass of milk, she raised her eyes and looked at him in a way he had never seen her look, pale and distant and knowing. All at once, a feeling came over him of standing and peering down into a deep, mossy well. He had never liked that feeling. He remembered how he had thought if he looked far enough down, he would see lakes of fire and brimstone, quivering red-hot.

"Daddy," she said, "I don't think I can eat."

He stopped. "You ain't hungry, honey?" he said, frowning at her. "You feeling all right?"

She shook her head, looking away out the window. "You don't have to bring me supper," she said. "Please, Daddy."

"You want to go on to bed?" He held the plate and glass and tried to make sense of what she said. "You're tired, I reckon, too tired to eat." And she looked tired, unwell, her skin toned grey when he saw her in the electric light, her strawberry hair so fragile and fine it seemed to be floating away from her head, strand by strand.

"Don't make it worse." Tears began to fall down her face. "I'm a whole lot worse. Oh, Lord." She lifted her hand and rubbed the tears away, but they kept coming back.

Holding to the things she did not want, Clement felt clumsy and useless. He remembered how Emmy used to eat the spaghetti circles lying on her stomach in front of the television, her hair in dog-ears quivering with her laughter. He wanted her to be fed. He was doing the best he could.

"Shh, now. Let's go upstairs, then." He put down the plate and glass, the milk sloshing a little, wetting the rim and dribbling onto the table. "We'll get you in bed." Her mouth began to wobble. He went over to her, to coax her from the chair. "It'll be better in the morning," he told her. "That's a girl." He gave her shoulder a squeeze.

She cried harder when he touched her, bowing her head and moving with her weeping. "Oh, Daddy," she wailed. It sounded like her mouth was full of water.

He had never known what to do when Ruth cried. It was no easier with his child.

"Come on, baby girl." He put his arm around her and nudged her forward. She dragged herself up, heavy with crying. "Don't blame you for feeling out of sorts. It's been a long time since you had you a rest in your own bed."

He walked slowly with her, guiding her toward the stairs, and she moved reluctantly. He was sorry this was how she felt, but he figured he was telling her what was right and best. She might not even know herself, just what was wrong.

"You'll be ready for breakfast in the morning," he said, and he thought it was a good word he gave her, even if he were not the cleverest of men.

But the morning found Emmy Foster sitting in the green recliner, her arms spread on the armrests, her head tilted back, her limp body covered with the pink log cabin quilt from her bed. She watched the curtains with drooping eyes. Clement went over and opened the curtains, but his daughter never moved. She only sighed and looked out the window.

"Couldn't you sleep at all, honey?" he asked. He was beginning to be unsure of many things.

She shook her head. "It isn't any use to me," she said, her lips quivering a little.

At breakfast, Emmy hardly ate five spoonfuls of the oatmeal her father brought her, her jaw slack as she moved the food about in her mouth. Dinner, supper, were much the same. Clement watched her from the kitchen doorway, and she never once turned her head towards him. In the evening, he went and opened the medicine cabinet and then stood and peered at the brown bottles, wondering if one of them could ease her any. That night, leaving Emmy in the recliner, Clement lay down in his bed and prayed that whatever ailed his daughter, the Lord would bless the singing in church tomorrow. Perhaps it would have the power to heal her fretful spirit. He clung to the covers while he slept.

The people of Beulah Creek woke into a cold morning, with the trunks of trees like great pillars of chilled stone and the earth brown and yellow with decay. As folks climbed into their cars or walked briskly to the church, they listened to the loud crunching and tapping of their footsteps. All other sounds in the world seemed to have been frozen into thick chunks of silence. Jack Hendrick passed Kenny McGuire, intending to speak, but their eyes dodged somehow. Jack thought Kenny's face was hard to look into that morning, like a pane of glass frosted over. Veeny Anderson clutched her black Bible and tried not to think of how empty it felt without the brightly colored bookmark tucked in its pages. Bundled into wool coats, their gloved hands burrowing deep into their pockets, chapped-faced worshippers gathered on the front steps of the Beulah Creek Baptist Church and huddled with their families, saying nothing, their backs turned to the sharp wind and to one another.

That morning, Emmy Foster walked with her father down the hill from their house, not knowing the cold, feeling the whispers hot inside her. She ducked her head away from the bright sky. She wanted to touch her father's hand as she walked, but she could not, any more than she could get out of her skin as she wanted, just to unbutton it and step free, the singing carrying her away. She had once been happy in her pale lavender dress. She felt the fabric against her legs, and her mouth trembled. The whispers were poison vines itching beneath her flesh.

When they came to the white clapboard building with its spire like a holy, uplifted spirit, Emmy put her eyes down onto the shriveled grey grass, a rattling leaf. The whispers made her see them and know her body was a collection of dust like the pale powder on the bookshelves she wiped with a rag. And yet she was hot with living, her cheeks flushed with the walk in the hot coat. She wanted to go into the cool, dark building. She wanted to bolt and run away to the hill, where she could put her face against the gravestones. She bit her lip. Perhaps no one would see her face and her calling, the secret deeds that seared behind her eyes.

Her father walked beside her and smiled at the backs turned towards him. He saw Jack Hendrick standing by the redbud tree in front of the church and called out to the other man, raising a hand in greeting. Jack looked at them with a tight face and said nothing. But he did not turn away his eyes as they approached. Emmy did not want him to find her magenta calling. She hung back a little.

"Morning, Jack," said Clement. His voice was the loudest thing in the town, seeming to echo across the mountains. Bits of faces glanced over at them, and then looked elsewhere. Emmy could feel the cold now. "How are things?" her father asked Jack.

"Well," said Jack, looking behind him quickly. "They've been better." He turned back to them. His words made pale patterns in the air.

Emmy felt the cold shadow of the church building climb across the ground towards her. She shuddered. She had done wrong to come.

"Noah sick or something?" said Clement. "I don't see him here."

Emmy could hear the turning down of her father's mouth, and it made her heart flat. She tried to imagine Noah lying in white sheets, his forehead dark and matted with his black hair. She was afraid of what was happening.

Jack shook his head. He looked tired. "God knows what's taken hold of him."

Her father raised his hand, stiffly, to the back of his head. "Don't rightly know what you mean by that." His fingers were thick, uncertain, as they touched his black and grey hair.

"I mean he won't be here this morning," said Jack. His face was pale dirt. Jack sighed and went on talking, and Emmy wished he would not. "Noah's going around at night carrying this piece of wood, a lampstand or some such thing he made. Nobody sees him out in daylight much, just wandering around the houses and out through the trees late at night." Jack glanced towards Anson Bledsoe's house and the bristling sticks that would be hydrangea bushes in the spring. "Lord, I don't know," said Jack, his hands on his hips. "The whole town's gone peculiar."

Emmy hunched her shoulders. She moved her mouth silently. She did not know what it would be to see Noah in the night, arms against the trees and purple. She twisted hair around her finger, over and over.

"You don't say." Clement rubbed the back of his neck. His eyes seemed cloudy and old.

"No, I do say," said Jack, glancing back towards the church steps. "It's about time somebody said it. There was that fellow . . . ." Jack winced and would not go on.

Emmy caught hold of her father's arm. "It's cold, Daddy."

"Which fellow?" Her father put his hand on her shoulder. It did not warm her.

Jack shook his head. "Some young fellow."

People were going into the church, and Emmy's eyes went after them. If she followed, she would enter the arms like a dove, and Jesus would come, and the whispers might leave her forever.

"Maybe it don't mean nothing," said Jack, "but I swear . . . ." He opened his mouth and shook his head.

Her hope was a cold light. "Can we go in, Daddy?" she said.

Her father turned towards her then, and his face was soft. She could not bear to see it for long. "Sure, honey," he said. Looking back at Jack, he said, "Emmy's feeling a bit poorly, so we'll go on and get us a seat. Good to see you this morning."

Jack looked at her. "Sorry to hear that, Emmy. Hope you'll be on the mend soon."

She tilted her head and looked at the mud and the yellow stubble. She nodded slowly. She was not sorry. The whispers told her what she was, the sound of fire licking over fresh wood.

Still, she went into the service meaning to pray. She sat on the dark pew and tried to make words. She moved her feet in circles and pressed her thighs together. She looked at the ceiling where the shadows tucked themselves into corners, crammed in close, waiting. There were rocks in her throat, pressing the words down, squeezing the life from them. All the while, Jesus watched her from the picture behind the pulpit, his face dreamy with heaven. She never lifted her eyes there. A small sigh came from her mouth, and she sat lower in the pew. She knew then that her heart was made of mountain, and that nothing else was any use anymore.

For Emmy, after that, the day passed in a cloud of white. She walked home with her father, moving her limbs in ways that wearied her. She returned to the recliner, where she looked through the haze of curtain and clamped her fingers in her lap. Low in her stomach was the calling, like lips of magenta, whispering. Pumpkin came once and rubbed against her leg, so she tucked her legs up beneath her skirt. The living room clock was ticking. It was a clock like a star, except the points were made of a bright, twisting metal, and it had always seemed rather fearsome to her. Slowly, the night began to come into the room. Her father wandered past her eyes sometimes, but she could hardly see him now. Then the lights went out in the house, and she was left behind.

She folded her arms and pressed against her middle. In the blackness, the chimes struck their strange, dainty chaos of tones, and the clock began to speak, saying not, not, not. When the singing came, low and open, it caught her in the midst of her body, like a hand reaching inside, peeling back the layers of her, until it dipped its fingers in the hot, sticky blood. She slid heavily to the edge, feeling the rub of the chair. She lowered her feet to the floor and raised her sturdy body into the air. She could smell the scent of living flesh, a smoky, salty smell. The clock knocked itself into her until she thought she would cry out. She must, she must give herself unto.

She stole the few, swift steps to the front door. The locks turned beneath her hands, because she knew the way. She had walked this way every night, for many a night. Once more Emmy cracked the door and passed through into the outer darkness. The cold scattered across her face and arms like bitter spray, like the wistful, erratic song of wind upon the chimes.

Crouching low, she went quickly through the shadows to the back of the house and the edge of her father's yard. Then, straightening, she walked towards the top of the hill. She sensed the spaces about her opening until she was far from every place. She folded her arms across her chest and rested her hands on her shoulders. The stars cried out, and the mountains replied, and his singing flared within her. Her calling was other than she had ever dreamed, full of pain, of bright fire, vermilion and violet. Down below, in the houses along the creek, she knew other girls were sleeping beneath flowered bedspreads like the Mullins twins, their lashes hushed upon their faces and their mouths pursed with rose petal dreams. But she, she could no more ask and be given. Her heart was made of mountain, of tombstone. She was as the daughter of Jephthah, she realized, for she was promised away before she knew. The calves of her legs tightened with the climb. She thought the word bewail.

Then she was slipping through the garden, the leaves nestling, slapping, trailing across her body, through the night all black and green. She slipped past the Greenberry house and peered up Sumac Hill into the branches spread for her. She began to climb more steeply, grasping for the handholds offered. She thought she would sink into the ground, pouring herself out, and yet it was not her, but all the ones she carried that night, the trickle of Greenberry blood, of Evans blood, that dropped at the last into her veins.

At last, gasping, she came to the place where her people lay. She could not see them, but she knew that beyond the grinning iron, the stones pierced up through the ground like shards of bone. She slipped inside. The singing here came flowing down over her, billows of gold and indigo splashed through with magenta. She did not know how she could hear such beauty. Her place quivered as she imagined it.

Then the song died upon the night. In the sudden quiet, she tried to see where he might be. The trees stood all around, and night creatures hurried in the shadows.

The gate creaked. Starting, she turned toward the sound.

"Are you afraid, Emmy?" Addison asked. "You said you were not."

She stepped nearer. "I'm here," she said. "I've come."

"I think it is in you to come." She could hear pleasure in his voice. "And I am glad of it. You are good to me, Emmy. You bring me good things. Not like the others." She thought he moved his hand, a gesture of disgust.

Walking closer, Emmy paused. "Malathy Joan is good to you." The thought of the woman with the long, sable hair and the ravaged voice made her swallow hard. "I know she is."

"Of course," said Addison. "Malathy." His words sounded farther from her, as if he had turned his head. Emmy waited for him to go on. He said, "She is sleeping now, but sleep is not with me tonight. So I came here to think awhile." He stopped again before saying any more. "I like to come here."

She found she was walking closer once more. Her skin crackled as she came towards him and his hands. He was a warm place in the dark, and his words sent warmth out to her. She stopped very close.

He brought his face back. "It is good, isn't it," he said, "for us to come together in a quiet place?"

Her shivers were surges of fire. They would come over her, and she would be changed, transfigured. She did not know why. Her eyelids fluttered shut. Low in her stomach, the slow throbbing pain began. She tensed against it, but felt herself ebbing away.

His voice held no laughter, only low tones of deep blue and an edge of slicing silver, as he said, "What is it you want to share with me tonight, Emmy?"

Her throat was wide and empty, and it reached all down through her. Her blood seethed the words of the dead, foaming into her mouth. All around her, the trees crossed themselves, branches bristling, their bodies forking ten thousand grey paths, both wide and narrow. She breathed so loudly that the town below would wake and the graves shudder open.

Her lips parted. "Every night," said the cold voice that whispered from her windpipe, squeezing her lungs. "Don't let it end."

He leaned over her, a dark body that burned from within, like her own dark body, and he spoke his words upon her neck. "This is why you come." The words each night like an incantation sank in her breast like coal-hot hooks, tearing into her heart until the muscle shredded, and she fell away inside herself, dwindling down into the bleakest corner. "And you will come each night you live, you sweet green girl, for you will want to find me here. There is no other, sweeter goodness than to give to help another's need."

When she was lifted, her flesh went hard. She thought she glimpsed a face, somehow, over his shoulder, a single, sharp image of cold eyes and rosebud lips, of strawberry hair very becoming, a woman's fleeting face, before Emmy crushed against him. He smelled of salt and hot, dry, summer wind. Her arms, her legs sprawled about him. Warm breath spurted against her cheek. Her skirts flowed back from her, and the palm of a hand cupped her, the fingers of a hand probed the hole between her legs until the waters ran out. Moaning, she was taken through the air, her back dug against the spiny bark of a tree.

He pushed her, and the magenta came radiant through her, like the wild, turning colors of his eyes, and she called for it, Jesus, sweet Jesus. She knew that he was beautiful and wicked, and still she took it unto herself, and yet not herself, crouching in the darkest, deepest corner of her skin, but unto another, the mother of the mountain that she was, that she would always be.

Again, again, the calling seared deep into her flesh. She smelled the burning, the sick, choking smoke thick in her mouth and nostrils. She gasped, she gagged, she gripped him, and her heart twisted to believe that her hope of heaven had been blighted for her breasts of granite, her caverns of limestone, her name of bloom and thorn, of bitter fruit, which instead had been bequeathed to her as an everlasting inheritance.

FLOOD

I

A dream troubled Noah Carpenter often as January and then February washed clear and cold and flashing through the landscape. He closed his eyes when he could no longer keep them open and found himself walking through the town in the middle of the night. In the dream, he passed heaps of stone and of rotted timbers that put him in mind of the bones of ships. He gripped the candlestick he had made and hunted for the dark thing with the crooked foot. He could hear it thumping about in the trees. It slapped and dragged, and he did not like the sound of it, the beat of its walk askew.

He followed the thing down into the dry, rocky, creek bed and over to the lower slopes of the hill where the Greenberry house stood. He understood then what it meant to do, as well as he could know such a thing in a dream, and began to climb. Where trees were felled long ago, and grass grew now in waking life, he encountered tomato vines and morning glories that twined about and snagged his legs. He ducked under pepper plants that had reared up tall as dogwood trees, while the sky turned shades of green and yellow, and the wind drove harder. He heard the creature rattling through the undergrowth and parted the leaves before him with one hand, watching for it to slip past.

Then the legs of his overalls felt damp, and that was when he looked down and saw the swell of water rushing fast at his heels. If he had not awakened already, he awoke from his dream in that moment, his breath quick and hard, unsteadying him.

On a night in late February, Noah had let his head fall forward, dreaming that very dream over the words of the Preacher in the Bible before him. Then his hand struck the table in his sleep, and he woke from the sound and the force. Very tired with looking, he looked then to know where he found himself. He took in the sight of the cupboard, the stove, the old clock shaped like a teapot that hung high on the wall above the old refrigerator. The house gave off silence like an echo that trembled about the sound of his waking.

He pushed back his chair. There was no need of sleep. Sleep told him only what he knew when waking. He closed his Bible and took up his coffee cup, dumping the lukewarm liquid into the sink. He figured it was the hour for him to keep watch.

Darkness lay just on the other side of that wall, he thought, and it hissed like the sea, rolling its waves out to distances he would never know. He listened, his mouth tight. It was a wonder to him that the great weight of the darkness did not fall upon them all, crushing them to dust, for high above Beulah Creek, all the stars and worlds in creation floated on a mighty tide of night. It was a piece of work he could not fathom.

Noah turned from the sink and reached for the candlestick he had set close by. The cool wood touched his hand like the worn knob to a door that was good to open. He lifted it from the table and carried it with him into the living room, where he took down his hat and wool jacket. He did not go walking to be cold or weary or faithless in some fool's fretting. That way led to madness, a chasing after wind. He drew the jacket sleeves onto his arms and reckoned it a careful thing, and not unpleasant, to walk the town in the night and watch it. This was not an answer he had reasoned out, but it seemed good and right to him to make it. In the Bible, the Preacher said a fool walked in darkness, and that might be true enough. But he figured he would keep his eyes in his head and see what there was to see.

The nights that Noah now walked with the candlestick in his hand belonged to days that leaned forward, taut and quivering with coming spring. In the dark, he breathed the scent of warming earth and the chill of starlight, the smell of new grass and the promise of rain. His eyes searched the shadows to watch the shiver of each bush as the wind passed. He knew the shapes of every shed and bungalow, plain enough in daylight for any to see, the old McGuire house made of stout logs, Bill Bledsoe's auto shop built of cinder blocks. But Noah thought them different in the night, places dark and unknown even to his hearing. He thought on this, too, that the town had not come there all of a piece, as it had seemed to him when he was a boy. Hands had built it with beams of wood, with tools bent to the purpose. As he walked, his boots disturbed fallen leaves, frail things that could not forget the cold, no matter what light touched them in summers to come. Dead leaves could easily be blown far away.

Always on his walks, Noah's steps brought him to the low bridge across the creek. He crossed it and climbed beside the gravel driveway to the Foster place. From the shelter of the porch, the chimes called to the thin smile of moon. The back of his neck chilled. Always he hesitated there for a time, the thing with dark fur scrabbling about in his chest. But he never climbed farther up the slope towards the Greenberry house. He turned and walked down again to Beulah Creek. He moved his right thumb down the curve of the candlestick, its shape gentle. She had a right to herself, to her own mind. He figured he could live so, though it was not to his liking. There were too many things he had not thought to give her, for he had had faith in the long, slow time before, and he had meant to make it last, the closeness of lives and hands and lips, words to say more.

Sometimes a bird sighed as he passed among the black trees. Sometimes a dog roused and barked in someone's yard. But late one night, Noah carried the candlestick along the road and caught sight of light in Jack Hendrick's store. The windows shone out like sunrise. Noah drew down his brows, and his boots beat more quickly upon the pavement as he shifted his grip on the candlestick. He did not know what midnight customer might be nearby. But as he came nearer, he could see Jack putting colored boxes on the shelves. Noah slowed then and, stepping to the door, tapped on the glass with his knuckles.

Holding a box of cereal in the air, Jack looked abruptly towards the door. "Hold on, there," he was saying, and then caught sight of Noah. Jack nudged the box into its place and came over, looking grey and slow to Noah's way of thinking. The lock clicked as Jack drew back the deadbolt, and the bells plinked against the dark. "Evening, there, Noah, or morning more like." Jack propped against door and frame. "I can open up if you're short on something."

"I saw your light," said Noah. He nodded his head once. "I thought I'd come take a look."

Jack turned his head and gazed at the shelves as though he had just now seen them himself. "Well," he said. "That was a good thought you had. I sure do appreciate you stopped." He paused and turned back. "I could do with some coffee. You're welcome to come on in a spell."

Noah reached for the door. "I reckon I'll do that." Jack stepped back, and Noah walked into the store. He considered the large brown box on the floor where Jack had been working. "I didn't figure you'd be stocking so late." The door closed with a tingle of bells.

"I didn't figure on it myself." Jack went over to the coffeepot. "Sleep is hard to come by in this weather, maybe. I don't know. This stuff needed doing, anyhow."

Noah stayed near the door. "How's Judy?"

"All right, I reckon." Jack was shaking his head slowly, as though in answer to some unasked question. "It beats all I ever seen. I can't keep bread on the shelves anymore without it molding, seems like."

Noah kept his eyes where Jack stood. "There's plenty whose blood has soured of late," said Noah. "And there's those that go looking for cause for it, where there may be or may be none."

Jack turned and looked from across the gleaming floor. "Lord help. I don't know who or what's causing every little piece of misery in this town, but some ungodly wretch broke into the church and took that picture of Jesus, the one Bobby Anderson give years back and him cold in the ground now. Tore Veeny up so bad they sent Betty to sit with her most of a day."

"I know it." Noah's brow tightened. "What's gone on here is what nobody ought ever even think, let alone do to one another. I'd as soon see it stopped."

"That's what you're out looking for now, whoever done it?" Jack eyed the column of wood in Noah's hand.

The light cut across Noah's face, sharp and silent from those days without sleep. "I reckon I'll see what I find."

Jack looked away. He fiddled with an empty Styrofoam cup. "I don't guess you've been up there lately."

"No."

The coffeepot gurgled and glared its small light. Jack tapped the cup against the counter. He hardly knew what he wanted to say. Her eyes were filled with looking, and she moved like a plume of grass in the wind. "Well. I don't know. Seems a shame to me. I don't know."

Noah studied the curve of light and shadow upon the good wood in his hand. His throat moved. "We've each of us got a right to our own mind, I reckon. Her, same as anyone. That's how the Lord made us."

Jack nodded. "He did, that's a fact," said Jack to the coffeepot.

They said no more until the coffee had brewed. Jack poured the steaming liquid into the Styrofoam cups. "You want anything in yours?" he asked Noah.

"I'll take it as it is," said Noah. He walked to Jack to take the cup and spread his fingers about the warmth and smell of it. It would be enough, he thought, and he would be satisfied to walk again in the dark. "Didn't come this way to trouble you none, but I won't be sorry to carry this with me."

"You're welcome to it," said Jack, stirring the sweetener into his cup of coffee. If any measure were to be taken in Beulah Creek, Jack allowed it could hardly be done more surely than beneath Noah's eye. A carpenter's hand would draw the mark in its right place. "There's somebody got to keep an eye on things around here," said Jack.

"I reckon I'd best turn my hand to what fits it these days." Noah turned his head and looked at the windows. The dark swelled against the building, a cold, swift river.

"Glad you stopped by," said Jack. "There's no trouble here, nothing bad wrong. That's a blessing, I guess."

Noah nodded. "I'll be on my way. You and Judy take care." He headed for the door.

"Watch yourself, now," said Jack, as Noah leaned into the door with his shoulder and pushed through into the darkness.

There were many in Beulah Creek who now asked and wondered, hissed and shook their heads whenever they spoke Noah Carpenter's name or else when they left it unspoken. Some looked at the empty place where Noah had sat in the pew and believed him to be wrestling with the devil. A few glimpsed him on his nightly errand. Late one night, Sarah Mullins tossed scraps from her back porch and saw the carpenter walking through the trees. Kenny McGuire drove home after coming off shift at the chemical plant down in Millsborough and briefly traced the carpenter in his headlights. Early one morning, Grandma Barnes opened her door to let out the dog and spied Noah coming up the road. The candlestick moved with the strong swing of the arm at his side, and his face refused to speak.

Noah always returned to his house after sunup. He took off his hat and wool jacket and placed the candlestick on the kitchen table. He made a slice of toast for breakfast and sat down to eat it with a small glass of grape juice. He washed the dishes afterwards in the sink and dried them. Then he went about his business as always, building for folks in the town. They asked him nothing, and that satisfied him. Still, when he saw their daylight faces and how they were fashioned, he minded the care that had been taken with each one. The sight of them kept him looking through the dark for what he did not know.

So it was that Noah found at last what he sought. An owl moaned on a night in March as he passed near the Mullins place. He was coming from the apple orchard at the edge of old Anson Bledsoe's land. He approached the back of the bungalow and remembered his labor on the banister inside, remembered a glass of iced tea on a thick summer day. Two little girls had peered down at him between the railings. Now beneath the moon, the backyard looked a desert place where no children ever came, where the swing set stood a hulking, long-legged creature in silver sands. He looked at the metal slide board bare in the starlight. As he neared the house, he saw a tricycle parked near the back door, the pedals poised in the midst of a ride.

He came around the corner of the house, where an oak tree groped towards the upstairs window, and its web of shadows stretched across the wall. Noah stopped. Someone stood there beneath the window, chanting softly, peering upwards amid the mottled darkness. Noah's neck and shoulders tensed. The figure snapped its head around to face him. Noah caught the movement of hair about the shoulders, and the voice disappeared. He could see the loose shirt and the jeans with gashes in the knees. He could see Addison's eye, wide and wary.

Noah felt a coldness in his throat, and his fingers froze tight to the candlestick. He had seen enough. "Reckon you'd best give your business." He took a step closer.

"I don't think you want to know it," said Addison.

Noah stood quite still then and looked at the young man. "I don't recollect telling you," said the carpenter, "to tell me what you think."

The lips twitched. "I'm walking in the dark. Can't anyone walk in the dark here but you?"

Noah felt the furred creature stir in the back of his mouth. He did not trust himself to move. "What do you want with these folks here?"

"I don't believe you care much for me," said Addison.

"I'm asking you." Noah had no use for this boy. There was no telling what Addison's hands had done.

"I don't believe you want me here or anywhere else."

"You've got no cause to be here." Noah crushed his fingers about the heavy wood. He had dreamed terrible things the night of the star, the last good night he had spent with her. He wished to God he could have that night again with her, before this abomination had ever come among them. "There ain't nothing in Beulah Creek for you. You'd best go back where you came from."

Addison shook his head. "I don't think so." The eye brightened. "I've found plenty to keep me occupied."

Noah grasped what such words might mean, and his arms went rigid. He did not like what next came to mind, the boy's head half gone and the shadows dripping down his face. Noah's hands were shaking. "Get," he said.

Addison hesitated, then took a step back.

"You come slinking down here again, I swear to God, I can't say what will be."

"I know." The young man nodded. "You could kill me. That would help you most, I'd think."

Noah watched him turn and walk away. Dead leaves whispered as Addison passed through them. Then the dark was still once more.

All at once, something tore loose inside Noah, something with deep roots and thick sinews. He had never felt such pain, such terrible anger. His throat burned, and his fingers gnarled up. He clamped his teeth together. He grasped the candlestick with both hands and drew back his arms to heave the thing into the side of the tree, but he could not hold onto it. He dropped the candlestick onto the ground, and it made a thud where it fell. He shut his eyes and leaned his head against the wall. He let himself breathe there awhile. The starlight crept slowly across the grass. The air moved upon his face.

At last, Noah opened his eyes. He bent and took up the candlestick. He walked back to his house and placed it on the table beside his bed. His back ached and the tender places between his ribs where he drew breath. Noah stretched himself out upon the quilt, one arm across his stomach, the other across his forehead. Then he slept. He slept without dreaming. He did not wake up for three days. The people of Beulah Creek looked at the closed doors and shutters of his house, their mouths open, their hands clasped together. They believed the end was very near.

II

One morning, Jack Hendrick trudged up the road to the store and realized the world had begun to move again. Birds scudded through the sherbet sky, and blossoms blew upon their stems. The set of Jack's face eased. The swing of his arms loosened. He waved to Chad and Sarah Mullins as they stood and talked by their red pickup truck. The grass glowed, and the wind grew warm as a living thing. As days went by, most in Beulah Creek found the air gentle against their bodies. It felt like floating to move. Veeny Anderson carried out her bedclothes and draped them on the line so she could carry them in again later to breathe the sweet, earthy aroma. It was comfort to her heart to hold such billowy piles in her arms. All about the town, people turned their faces towards the sun to dry the sleep from their eyes. They reached their hands into the dirt, hoping to stir up life into the roots of things.

But high upon the hill overlooking Beulah Creek, the season did not turn as it should. The Greenberry house sat in the midst of a land bleached and browned, beneath a colorless dawn and a grey dusk. The house itself looked strangely weathered, as though waves of sand had pounded against the boards for many days and many nights. The garden had fallen into dust.

Inside the house, Malathy Joan lay upon her bed and looked at the wall, her sight marred by a mist that drifted through her eyes. At times the wall faded, so that she could almost see the downward slope of the hill beyond. The skin of her face felt tight or loose, as though it no longer fit her. When her fingers touched where her face should be, she touched flesh and bone, but was not entirely certain of the memory.

"Jess," she whispered. "You have been here. I know you are not far."

Malathy Joan stretched out her cupped hand. She was not afraid to wait for what would come to her. It was not peace that came. She knew no name for it, only that she blurred. She was inhabited by another woman's life, the distinction between them nearly gone. In her remembrance, she rose from her rocking chair in the night at the sound of footsteps on the back stoop. Her husband was away, and the one who came could fill her as nothing and no one else could. But somehow she was also the woman who had once picked tomatoes from the vine, each firm fruit a token of a sun-ripe day she had lived at Beulah Creek. Malathy Joan looked at the palms of her hands, dark and crumpled. She could not say what she saw there now.

At times, she roamed the house like a famished beast gnawing the stubble of fields. Her white nightgown trailed against her ankles. Her heart labored as she turned her head about, uneasy. She had lost something, it seemed, and she remembered only that she craved it. Her hands fumbled at the objects on the mantel. She had kept a precious thing there, and the cool feel of silver passed through her head until it was nearly a taste on her tongue. As she searched, something stared at the back of her head. Sometimes the thing watched from her left shoulder. She could not think even to curse its name.

Addison would approach her then and grasp her shoulders. "What is it?" he asked her, his voice close upon her face. "What is it you've taken to seeking?"

She shook her head. "I believe it is seeking me."

"Don't let it trouble you," he said. "It will find you if it wishes, I should think."

He stood behind her and kneaded her shoulders slowly. She reached her hand to touch his and closed her eyes. Her heart constricted. She glimpsed a memory of herself touching another hand in just such a way. That hand had kept her well, once, in the distant city. It had dressed her and brought her beautiful things. It had worn a ring not hers.

But the thought unraveled and dropped in tangles at her feet. She returned to her bedroom, stepping over the knots and loops of bedclothes. She did not mean to forget. Past and present, forgetting and remembering, all rose up together within her, and she breathed it all in, as fragrant as lilacs.

One afternoon, Malathy Joan stirred in bed at the sound of something beating at the front door. It beat, and then beat again.

She sat up. She pushed back her hair. Still the door pounded.

She saw herself climb from the bed. The floor stretched five miles to the door, and she walked them barefoot, her flesh icy. Somehow she remembered what was about to happen. She would put her hand to the door and pull it open. A young girl, the midwife's daughter, would look at her with eyes that knew. The girl would spit words at her to sting, choking her with their poison. The girl had crouched behind a tree in the dawn and watched as one man bludgeoned another to death. Malathy recalled she would stand before the girl and listen, and her mouth would not be able to open as she heard. She would drop away into the outer darkness and know herself destroyed.

She saw herself place her hand upon the doorknob. It turned, and the door let in a stunning light. She lowered her head and shielded her eyes. She blinked and peered to see what had come to her.

"Look at you." Grandma Barnes stuck her crooked finger in Malathy Joan's face. "I've seen shameful in my day, but, Lord, I'm looking at it now."

Malathy Joan squinted and tried to find the child there. She heard the old voice cracked like the shells of walnuts. She could see the stooped figure dark and scarcely knowable in the flood of sunlight. She felt something tug in the bottom of her stomach.

"I remember you," she said, speaking both from some distant memory and from the moment right before her. Malathy's eyes looked out of black holes, and her face had shrunken into bone. "You've come to tell me something I've no wish to hear."

Grandma Barnes grunted. "I ought to drag you out here and beat you before the Lord."

From the front step, the black dog howled. Malathy Joan pressed her trembling hand to her forehead. "What have I done?"

The old woman twisted up her mouth. "Ain't it plain enough for you? I wouldn't set foot on this God-forsaken place, laboring all the way up here and it nigh killed me, but I've got to say my mind." Grandma Barnes knocked the end of her cane against the porch. "I won't stand by and watch that Carpenter boy go to ruin without saying what's got to be said."

Malathy Joan felt her arms chilling. "Noah? Is he well?"

"What do you think?" Grandma Barnes squinted at her. "Is a man that's been wandering through the woods at midnight a body that is well?"

Her hands fell at her sides. "No. Is that what's come to him?" The light stirred in her eyes. "I am sorry for it."

"But not hardly sorry enough."

A taut string quivered in her chest. "I . . . can't see what I should do." The carpenter would not surely come for her now.

"You've got the eyes for seeing." Grandma Barnes jabbed her cane close to Malathy's bare foot. "But that ain't mine to tell you. You know it, and you'd best find it out."

"I can see well enough to know what you did here before," she said. "I know, long ago, what you came to say."

At first, the old woman did not answer. "I expect you do," said Grandma Barnes then. "And if you don't come on down from here, you'll see quick enough what more is coming."

Malathy Joan looked out at the withered land and marveled that it did not crack open beneath the hot, white light. Her breast burned. "I suppose I'll know the whole of it soon," she agreed.

"What's the trouble here?" Addison spoke behind her.

The dog growled, a long, low rumble like a coming storm.

"You," said Grandma Barnes. "Whoever you are, you are nothing but."

"There's no trouble," said Malathy to Addison. But her smile died before it reached her eyes. She thought of what had come to Noah.

"It doesn't sound that way to me," said Addison.

"We two are of a mind, then," said Grandma Barnes. "You'd best take yourself on out of here. Either the way you come or on down the road, it don't matter. She can come to my house, get herself together, but you'll get no welcome there from me."

"But I have what I want here," said Addison. "It makes me think of fine old times." He stepped forward. "I can help you down the hill if you need, granny."

"Don't you touch me," said Grandma Barnes, pulling back a step. "Lord, I'm done with you." The old woman set her shoulders between herself and

Malathy Joan. "You go on and carry on how you will. But I've spoke, and I ain't staying anymore."

Malathy listened as the old woman creaked and bumped away from her front door and down into the grass. It could be the sound of a house settling into the earth.

"I'm glad you came," said Malathy, turning to Addison. And she was glad. Her heart felt covered over with dust and dark webs. "I didn't want to say anymore."

"Did that old woman bother you?" Addison moved aside so she could pass by him. "You shouldn't listen to her talk if it worries you."

"No." She walked back into the house. The shadows fell across her. She clutched them close like crocheted folds, and still she shivered. "She doesn't bother me. But I'm wearied with this place, tired of so very much."

She crossed into the bedroom. Her chest rose and fell as the sigh of wind in winter. Something looked through her head. It walked just behind her like the dark shape she cast. She wondered vaguely where Addison went and when he came again. The lilacs filled her head, and she stretched among the covers. She longed to be at peace. The curtains parted within her, stirring slowly. She let the wind carry her far.

But the wind carried the days along, too, and the day came finally when the wind changed. Down in Beulah Creek, the wind darkened and strove with the trees. Cold drops of rain spattered against gravels and shingles. The dog moaned where it lay on Grandma Barnes's living room floor. The dog got up and trotted to the window, where it stood and watched with a quizzical expression. Grandma Barnes knitted near her table lamp in the living room and listened as the dog whined. Her needles clicked, and the red yarn locked together, held fast like a clasp. She heard the hiss in the rain. Most folks had deaf ears, but the wind had a bitter sound, and she knew to dread it. She reckoned it had come to do violence.

The wind blew likewise against the Greenberry house, but there the air fell dry and stinging against the weatherboards. Malathy Joan could touch nothing in the house without feeling a crackle upon her fingertips. She drew breath and let in the wandering spirit of Jess Greenberry. She let go her breath, and it smelled of lilacs. Her limbs glistened, and her forehead burned.

On the night that the ghost woman came at last to clasp her fingers and lead her away to Sumac Hill, Malathy's hand lay empty upon the bed. She felt the air move against her skin, and the chill felt good to her. She opened her eyes then and knew, as she had not before, that Addison had not lain beside her for nights without number. She sat up. The heat of her flesh smothered her. Her heart began to beat high in her throat. She looked into the dark. She caught the shimmer of silver and smelled purple stirring in the room.

"Jess," she said. "Where have you taken him?"

The ghost woman took shape before her. Jess stood as firm and clear as a living woman but could be seen in any darkness. Her dress was russet, and she wore an opalescent brooch. She clenched her left hand as though she clutched something slight and small. Malathy wondered what it could be.

"Am I to be left with nothing?" said Malathy Joan. Her hair stuck to her face and neck, her body dripping with warmth. "What more have you done?"

Jess Greenberry's parted lips smiled. The pretty face laughed without sound. Cold eyes fixed upon Malathy Joan with a light that could have made blood run down the walls and congeal as ice.

"Please," said Malathy. She stretched her arm out upon the bedclothes, her palm upturned. "Show me."

Jess reached down and wrapped her fingers about Malathy Joan's wrist. The cold sucked away sight and breath. She gasped and clutched her throat and found that she stood outside her back door. The hot wind tore at her pale nightgown, and her hair streamed out like storm clouds rising. The silver figure of a woman walked before her into the trees.

Malathy followed almost before she knew. Branches swung above and all about her. Flashes of light swept across the sky. A stone pierced her foot, but she hobbled on, smearing dirt into the wound and blood upon the earth. Rumblings came from deep within the mountains. Still she walked after the ghost woman. Her legs strained. She reached for tree trunks to guide her upward. The claw of one tree grabbed her sleeve and ripped into her arm. Jess reached for nothing. The wandering spirit only lifted her skirts as she climbed.

Pushing back the boughs from her path, Malathy Joan came at last to the top of Sumac Hill. Light cracked overhead. She glimpsed the frail bones of a wrought-iron fence, and gravestones stood beyond. Jess stopped a few steps before her. The ghost woman turned her head, and her eyes were shrill against the dark. Malathy Joan did not know what Jess had done, but her chest was wracked with terrible rhythms. She wanted the wandering woman to go down into the earth to take her everlasting rest.

Before she could cry out to the spirit to ask and know, the world crashed into brightness. Two figures writhed together against the rough flesh of a tree in the center of the graveyard. She saw arms and legs and jeans and skirts. The man and woman were coupling madly. They were near enough to her that she could see the man's hair blown about his shoulders by the wind. Then the dark swallowed them. She stared where they had been.

Again the light showed two figures bucking, heedless. She stood and tried to hold her heart within her. The girl twisted her head to one side, and Malathy Joan saw the girl's gaping mouth, her eyes wrenched shut. For the space of a single breath, it was Jess's face she saw. Then she knew it clearly for the face of Emmy Foster.

Malathy spun about, her hand to her mouth, knowing herself deeply wronged. She began to run down the hill and grabbed at the branches as she passed. Cold, fierce grief followed her. She placed her injured foot wrong, and her leg buckled. She slid onto her back, jarring head and body. The thunder roared through the mountains. She pulled herself up again and ran. Rain gushed from the sky. Her nightgown shriveled about her, and her hair poured down her back and shoulders. She skidded between the trees and pounded the final steps to her kitchen door. She tore it open and threw herself inside. Only then did she stop. She stood and dripped upon the hardwood floor. She clutched her forehead as she cried.

"What am I to do?" she whispered. She shook her head. "What am I to do?"

She wept until her heart turned to rust. When she lifted her head at last, she knew that all she had believed, all she had done, had been in vain. Her fingers had merely stirred up dust and let it fall again to the earth. She limped into the front room. Her foot stabbed pain up her leg. The rain beat upon her roof, and the wind keened as it passed. She would lift her fingers no more, for Addison or for Emmy Foster or for any other soul before God. She lowered herself into the rocking chair. The wood creaked. She would move the chair beneath her and let the world go on as it would. It did not have the power to move her anymore. She was finished with it.

III

The skies fell upon the Greenberry house. Wind and water dropped without mercy. The stranger woman rocked in Jess's chair and let the sound of the torrent wash through her. Piece by piece, it would bear her away. She rested her hands lightly on the arms of the chair. Her hair tumbled down her shoulders and into her lap, as the blood moved beneath her skin and traced the map to her heart. She did not know what would become of her neighbors when the waters began to rise. She hardly remembered their faces anymore. Out of the great holes of her eyes, she watched the window and waited for what would come.

She did not know the hours that passed by her door. Then she heard someone enter the house through the kitchen. The back door closed quietly as though moved with care. Next the floor creaked beneath footsteps that shifted around the table and towards the kitchen doorway. Her fingers tightened. She pressed her lips together, and they were still. The steps neared the threshold and then crossed into the front room.

"Don't come any closer to me," she said to the one who walked behind her. Her voice rasped on the air like the words of the dead.

The floor lay silent. The walls said nothing.

"I want you to leave this house," she said. Her words were cold and gliding. "I can't harbor you here anymore."

"Something's happened," said Addison. "You don't speak like yourself. You're mistaken."

Her stomach wrenched. "No," she said. "You're mistaken. I saw you."

She turned her head to look at him. He stood with his hands open. Light shone from his hair. Her legs tensed, but she did not let them lift her from the chair. "I know what you've done, Addison. What is worse, you've known it, too. I don't need to know anything more about you." From a very deep place, she spoke somehow for Jess Greenberry, also, as she put behind forever what should never have been before her. She was pained and satisfied to say what she said. Though her body had grown hollow, her soul drifting like fog on a mountainside, beneath her words lay sharp peaks of granite.

The color left Addison's face. "I don't know what you saw," he said. "But I can explain it to you. I think you'll understand." He lowered his hands. "Your heart is gentle. It's made for understanding."

She looked at him, at his light and his hair and his beautiful skin. More than anything, she regretted that she did not understand. Now she never would. She turned away. Her hair dropped between them, and she was alone.

"There's nothing you can say, Addison. I'm sorry. It's best that you go now." He was quiet a moment. "I'm sorry, too," he said.

She watched the rippling curtain of rain. It blew past the window and spattered the ground. The footsteps began once more. They trailed away from her into the kitchen. She shuddered, and she shut her eyes. That was all. The back door opened and closed. She rocked her chair. She felt the curved slats cut into her back and thought of her ribs grinning, thought of the teeth in her jaw.

The people of Beulah Creek, too, began to think of death, of cold hands and dark wings aloft, though they could not know the stranger woman had sent away the handsome young man and now sat and waited for the world to fall down. As the Greenberry house creaked and groaned beneath the rain, Noah Carpenter pulled on his boots and rain slicker and walked down to look at the creek. He shook his head, his mouth severe. He saw an ugly creature that roiled its way through the town, swollen from feeding on the bitter snows. The water churned frothy and brown. It spewed up now and again from its banks. It carried things away, bits of trees, someone's trash. He figured it was after something more.

Noah lowered his head against the wind and went back to his house. He closed the door, but the sound of rain seeped into everything in the town. He wondered how long it would be before the walls rotted and the ground gave way. He hung his rain slicker near the door but kept on his boots.

In his bedroom, he opened a drawer and took out the weather radio. He placed it on the table at the center of the living room and flicked it on. He listened as he brought from the rooms of his house a flashlight, the Bible, a loaf of bread, a plastic jug of water, and the candlestick. He set them each one by the radio. The machine droned on, foretelling fearful things. They would not be seen in Beulah Creek for some hours yet, but he reckoned he would do well to be ready. He checked the clock above the mantel to know the time. He dropped the keys to his van in the pocket of the rain slicker.

All over town, people watched the rain fall and felt something cold and terrible rise up into their throats. They called the children to play close at hand. They gathered up photo albums and jewelry cases. Some spoke to friends on the telephone or kin who lived far from water and asked after a dry bed for a few days. They did not know, as they hurried, that it was the year that the rain would fall on all alike. It fell on Beulah Creek and the Greenberry house. It pelted the gravestones nestled by the church house and those planted high on Sumac Hill. Some whispered of the stranger woman who consorted with devils and of the cruel winter that had descended upon the town. Some declared it would be the day of God's judgment on them all. Most huddled with their arms around one another and peered at the tiny glimmering drops that fell from the sky.

High above the creek, Emmy Foster knotted her fingers in the folds of her pink curtain. She stood by her bedroom window in her father's house and watched the grey water sink into the earth. It dripped inside her ribs. When Pumpkin bumped his head against her calf, the cold went up her leg. She had buried Jesus out there in the yard, the holy face she had lifted from the wall of the church, but the water would make him rise again. The power trembled in the air and in the ground. She felt it growing in her belly. Jesus had spoken words in red that told her of death and the life it brought. Her hands were altogether wicked, but she knew that Jesus loved her still. She had taken his face and buried it to keep him near her always.

She opened her fingers from the curtain and crouched to gather Pumpkin in her arms. He allowed himself to be wrapped about with her bones and flesh. She held him against her chest. He was warm and shook with a low, rattling hum of contentment. She lowered her face against his orange fur. Her heart felt alive, beating against him, and it frightened her to know her life was kept there.

"I love you, kittycat," she whispered. She had not held him in a long time. It was the closest thing she knew to praying just then, for her mouth would not let her anymore. Pumpkin mewed in reply, and she was thankful.

She let Pumpkin go after a time. He made a high-pitched sound and dropped away onto his four feet. She stood slowly and watched him trot over to the bed. Her mouth wanted something sweet. She went to her bedroom door and slipped into the hallway. She was stepping down the stairs towards the kitchen and the refrigerator when the telephone began to chirp. She paused and leaned over the railing. The telephone stopped. Her heart kept going.

"Hello?" her father said. "Well, howdy there, Noah. Haven't heard much from you lately."

Emmy curved her fingers where they rested about the railing. Even here, the rain made her damp and cold. She stood upon the steps and kept her breath hushed.

"Now, that don't sound good, all this rain still to come. What are they saying?"

She could hear how her father's face would look, the crease between his brows, the sag at the corners of his mouth. She was sorry. But a dull pain began in her stomach. She felt the slow throbbing come and knew what she wanted now. The calling stirred awake, a pulse of magenta, coming unto, unto.

"Well, we've got us some room. It ain't no fancy motel, but folks are welcome to what we've got. You bring whoever don't have no place to go." He paused. "That's my thinking. The creek won't wash us out, not unless it's the day of reckoning, in which case it's our time anyhow. You go on and round folks up, and we'll be looking for you all. All right then."

She heard the click of the telephone. Her father said nothing else. She lifted her fingers and edged back against the wall. She felt the dark breathing outside. It passed as a whisper in the grass. She put her hands to her throat. She could not stay here with all those people. They would look at her and see the sickness eating her insides. She vomited sometimes, when she imagined black like blood creeping and growing within her.

"Emmy?" her father called. "Can you come down here a minute, honey?"

She hesitated. Then she shifted forward. "Here I am, Daddy." She came quickly down the steps, but there was no joy in her walk. "What is it?" she asked. She knew that she lied. She lied every day that she was awake. She thought of Jesus's face slimed with mud, and her heart pinched.

Her father walked towards her from the kitchen. "That was Noah who called. He said the creek's up and still coming, and there's people needing a place to stay until the water goes back down. I told him we'd take them here, since it's not too likely the water's going to come this high. We'll be all right here. So I reckon we'll put them somewhere, spread out some blankets and all. Can you help me a little, so we can look out for these nice folks?"

"I can if you want me," she said. She clasped her hands together over her stomach.

He smiled at her. "That's a girl," he said.

So Emmy helped pull quilts out of closets and old trunks. The fabric felt cold, a little filmy in her hands. She counted cheerful cans of soup in the cabinets. She made sure they had a red box of powdered milk. She even helped Clement push the sofa and recliner to the corners of the living room and carry the coffee table upstairs into her father's bedroom. She remembered nothing of what she did. Her hands sweated, and she felt the shrill need that told her she should go. It stabbed up into her like the fangs of a serpent.

"I'm going out to the shed," said Clement. "I think there's an old sleeping bag out there."

She lifted her face like sunlight on a distant valley. "I can go, Daddy," she said.

"Well, all right, honey," he said. "Be sure to take the umbrella, though."

She held to the black umbrella as she stepped out the front door. The chimes splashed music among the glistening water, but the tones seemed dark and hollow. She walked down the steps and into the yard. She opened the umbrella and held it high, and rain scattered from the metal points. She headed around the house to the shed, ducking a little.

The day had fled across the mountains and left nothing behind. The earth sucked at her shoes as she stepped across the watery surface. She heard and felt it more than she saw it. She thought how the ground had swallowed the face of

Jesus, and she thought of it swallowing her bare legs down into the mud. Her place came peeping open, feeling, seeking. One fist clutched her denim skirt, while the other held the rain off with the umbrella. She approached the shed and was fumbling to take the key from her skirt pocket. She stuck the umbrella handle in the crook of her arm, when light appeared behind her.

Emmy turned and saw two bright lights cut through the black and falling water. She heard the loud, gruff snuffling of a motor and the chunk and crunch of tires among the gravel. The lights swung towards the house, and the noise of the tires subsided. She felt her heart squeeze into her throat. The air had no place to move. She could not go back. She could not face them. The air scorched the passages in her nose until she thought her whole face had become fire.

She heard the sound of a car door opening and closing. Her body jolted. She heard her father's voice and then the slow, steady words of Noah Carpenter.

She shrank close to the wall of the shed and crept back along it, away from the house. She could not let Noah see her. Her thoughts crawled like beetles in a sodden stump. He would look at her out of his angry face, and she could not look back at him without falling away in terrible pain.

She turned her body up towards the long slope of hill she could not see. Her father's umbrella dropped from her fingers. She turned and pushed herself through the rain. It poured down her blouse and skirt. She pressed her hands to her temples, and the water ran down her wrists. She bent over and trampled through the mud and the grass. Her hair blew about her in stinging confusion, but she knew where she ran. She was called to go.

Her legs dropped her feet against the ground frantically. Her clothes became heavy with water. She could taste the cold and smell the rain. She could see the dark shape of the Greenberry house huddled before the height of Sumac Hill. Rivers of mud flowed where gardens had been, and splashes striped her legs. She passed the house, empty of light, and fled among the trees. She climbed with every part of her, pulling, pushing, grasping to get her closer. Branches sang strange tones upon the wind as they reared and swooped above her. She burst at last into the clearing where the dark smiles of iron and stone turned upon her. She raced to the fence and clutched the rusting rails. They smelled like her blood dripping from broken skin.

She listened. "Where are you?" she called. She sought the shifting darkness. The world hissed and sighed about her. Her legs trembled. Her heart shook the fence she grasped. Tender magenta spilled upon the dark, oozing water, trickling sweet. Her hands stung, and then she was crying. The calling tore her so desperately. She put her hands to her stomach. She shrieked, and her heart burst into fire. He did not come. He had left her, and his absence stabbed like the fearsome, twisting spikes of the clock that spoke not, not, not. She had neither his body nor his voice nor his words, no green garden, no fine shining morning, but only the epitaph of Jess Greenberry cut deep into her heart. Her mouth was full of her hair and the wet of her sobbing. She had no hope of anything more.

After a time, she straightened. Sure then of what she should do, she turned about from the graveyard and ran down the hill. There was only one face she could look upon now. It was shaped of sad knowing. It would look upon her and love her. Encircled by the brittle bones of Malathy Joan's arms, Emmy would know the answers to all that she asked, know the place she was meant to be. The wild pounding of her legs carried her to the back door of the Greenberry house. She caught herself against the door and beat the palm of her hand upon the wood.

"Help!" she said. "Help me, please!"

Her words dropped to the ground and bobbed in a muddy puddle. Emmy stood and listened to the swish of rain against the darkness. She did not believe what she heard. The answer she received was none. Her heart jerked so fast and violently she thought it would crash to a stop, and she would die there on the doorstep.

"Malathy?" she said. "Malathy Joan?"

She stepped down and stumbled around to the front of the house. The world was drowning in the flood of dark that fell from the sky. Emmy staggered onto the porch. Her mouth quavered.

"Please," she whispered. "Your name is so beautiful. Don't go away from me forever." She did not know how she could ever follow. Mary Magdalene walked a long and broken road, sharp with thorns, her long toes bare. "I can't be like you," she said. "I can't."

She lifted her hand and knocked. The noise went deep within the house. "I'm Emmy," she said. "I want your help so very much. Please let me in." She leaned towards the door and hoped for answer at last.

Inside the house, the stranger woman rocked. Her legs knew no motion but the sway of the chair, and her ears knew no sound but the roar of the storm. It was her heart that heard the voice of the child. Her fingers curved about the arms of the chair. Her heart could hold no more. She was covered in dark remembrance as the fall of her hair, as the drape of shawl about her shoulders. She had tended a house of poor wanderers who had all trespassed against her kindness and care. She would not open her door, not to this one, not on this night. The world outside would pass as it should, and in the end, it would take her, too. The chair moved her body. Her face never changed.

Emmy heard the strange creaking beyond the door. It echoed across the mountains to the end of the earth. It was the creaking of trees and uprooting of houses, the unhinging of doors and drowning of roads. It was the destruction of many things. She sank slowly to her knees and knotted her hands against her stomach, bending over. Her hair slapped against the porch. Her mouth opened, strung with frail ropes of water, but she could make no sound. She shook. Her back heaved. Malathy Joan had cast her out, not welcoming, not wanting her. She looked at the old boards. Her name was nailed to them for an everlasting inheritance. It was the ugliest thing she had ever known.

Sometime after, Emmy Foster rose from the porch and wandered in the night where no one could tell. She left a wet place upon the boards. The grass rippled on the slope. The town of Beulah Creek began to wash away.

IV

The dark waters of Beulah Creek surged beneath the small bridge that suffered the Fosters each day to reach the road that led from town. That night, as Clement readied his house for guests and Emmy still carried key and umbrella out to the shed, Noah Carpenter drove his van across the bridge, bearing the people who had no place of refuge to the Fosters' home. The headlights pierced a path through the rain and the blackness. Inside the van, the refugees huddled together, while the dark beyond the windshield filled with voiceless cries riding the winds to the clouds above.

Against the people of Beulah Creek the night was rising, boiling forth from the creek bed. It would swallow cars and couches. It would disgorge its refuse, knocking down backyard swings and pouring filth through flower beds. Still the rain fell and kept falling on the saddest, most grievous night the town had ever known. Nearly all who watched it unfold told the terrible story afterwards, as the tale was told for generations to come, how the stranger woman had come to Beulah Creek in the fall of the year to make their homes a desolation through her sin and her folly.

As Noah's van stopped with the passengers at the Fosters' house, a door opened welcoming light onto the darkness. It was precious to stand, blessed for the riders to burst from the narrow place where they had been and hurry for shelter. Noah and Clement carried old Anson Bledsoe into the house and helped Grandma Barnes and Veeny Anderson down from the van. Grandma Barnes's black dog leaped out and sprang to the porch in a flurry of mud and spray. There it stood, ears cocked, until Grandma Barnes stepped vigorously up the steps and gave it a nod. "Dog," she said, and it sat and regarded her.

The Mullins twins tensed and clutched their mother's hands for protection as they passed the tall, black animal. Their father had to work in the lowlands that night, away from them.

Clement stood in the middle of the living room and reached for each person who entered his house. "Come on in," he said. The room was bright and dry. Old Anson Bledsoe lay upon the gold sofa, the sticks of his hand gnarled about the white sheet. Quilts piled upon the footstool. The television flickered, and silent weathermen moved like giants across the continental United States, which swirled with clouds.

Clement gestured to an empty place against the wall near the kitchen doorway. "Veeny, Sarah, you-all just put your things where you want them. You're welcome to anything I can get you." He did not smile, but his broad face was mild, and his hand quite solid and well-meaning on the hands and shoulders of others. "Glad to help out however I can. Emmy's gone for an extra sleeping bag, and we've got food and quilts enough, I reckon." He looked toward the door. "You need me to carry anything, Noah?"

Noah shook his head. He carried the strap of a duffel bag across his shoulder and the handle of a suitcase in each fist. "This here's the last of it," he said. He placed the suitcases on the floor and turned to close the door.

"Don't lock up just yet," said Clement. "Emmy's bringing something from the shed out back."

Noah nodded and pushed the door shut. The black dog lay outside upon the porch, its head lifted, its eyes upon the wind chimes blowing frantic music.

Clement brought out glasses of ice and filled them with water, tea, and Coke. He gave them to whoever asked, and most were glad to have them, for empty hands now had something to hold. Veeny sat down in the recliner with her purse firmly in her lap. Grandma Barnes perched on a straight-backed chair that had been brought from the dining room table and took out her knitting. Miranda and Melinda Mullins knelt on the carpet and walked their Barbie dolls quietly through the tall, orange grass.

Alone in the kitchen, Noah stood by the window and listened to the burble of brewing coffee and the slap of rain on the roof. He pressed one hand against the countertop and folded the other about the handle of an empty mug. The window faced the long slope towards the Greenberry house, and he peered as far as he could see in the dimness. He was thinking of things he could not shape into words. The town was being torn from them, floating away down the mountains. He could turn his hands nowhere to do any good. It was hard to be parted from what he had come back to Beulah Creek to claim, and he could make no sense of it happening. His eyes moved slowly through the dark, and his thoughts moved more slowly still, so that it took him several moments to realize he was looking at the shed behind the Fosters' house. It appeared shut and unmoved. He could not tell that anyone was there.

He leaned his face closer to the window. The flesh beneath his brows fell into shadow. He lifted a hand and pulled a fold of the drapes until the light from the kitchen vanished from the backyard, and the image of his face disappeared from the glass. He figured he ought to know what he saw and what he didn't see. It was too soon to speak, otherwise. His eyes narrowed. He could tell the shape of the shed. He could tell the long hill beyond and the dark places nearer to the sky where the Greenberry house stood below the bristling slopes of Sumac Hill. If someone wandered through the rain, he could not see it.

He turned from the window and the kitchen countertop. His boots made weak, flat sounds upon the linoleum as he crossed to the doorway. He stopped and looked at Clement handing a glass of iced tea to Sarah Mullins. Noah turned over the words he would say, hefting them, thinking of the shapes they held. He was pleased with none of them.

"Clement," he said at last. The older man raised his eyes. Noah touched his fingers to the door facing. He felt it cool and steadying. "I don't see her out there."

All the faces looked to Noah. Grandma Barnes clicked her needles, her lips pinched. Pumpkin warbled.

"Well, now, that's true," said Clement. "She hasn't come in." His brows pushed together. "She's coming around the house now, I'd say. She can be a woolgathering little thing, though it sure seems a devilsome night for that."

Clement walked towards the front door. He opened it, and the sound of the weather blew into the room, chill and dripping. The chimes danced in everyone's ears. Grandma Barnes's dog barked. Grandma Barnes hissed and lifted her head. "Hush!" she called, and the dog was silent.

"Emmy, honey?" said Clement out into the rain. "You need to come on, now."

Everyone watched Clement's back, the set of his shoulders as he leaned towards the expectation of his daughter's voice. No one spoke. No footsteps came upon the porch. The water rushed headlong to the ground, and the night bubbled and oozed.

Clement stepped out the door, even as Noah left the kitchen and crossed the living room. Miranda and Melinda gaped up at him.

"Emmy?" said Clement, louder. "Get over here to the porch, honey. We're waiting on you."

Noah reached the front door. Clement half turned, glancing back over his shoulder. His face looked wide and open with a bewildered wonder. "I guess I'll take a look out back," he said. "Might be she had some trouble somehow, locking or unlocking that door. Or maybe she dropped the key and can't find it," he said as he turned and walked away.

Noah said nothing. He did not like to reckon about other folks' doings unless he had good cause. He took his rain slicker and his flashlight from the chair by the door where he had left them. He followed Clement across the porch. At the sound of Noah's boots, Clement looked back again. His eyes flicked to the flashlight in Noah's hand, then, startled, to Noah's face. "You don't reckon we'll need that?"

The black dog moaned. It was stretched out upon the porch, its head resting on its paws.

Noah shrugged. "I figured it might be good to carry." His face unsettled the older man, with grim lines like the scowl of rock beneath the soil.

Clement's eyes were troubled. "Lord, she's just out back, here," he said. He turned and headed down the steps. "Not listening to me." The chimes beat together, feverishly merry.

They walked through the yard. Noah cut the flashlight on with his thumb, and a broad span of light went before him. His boots disturbed the watery ground, spattering up the legs of his overalls. The earth tugged back at his boots, but he stepped as deliberately and as quickly as he could. He wondered if some ragged, crippled creature, like the one in his dream, had crept through the rain to linger by the Fosters' shed. The mud sucked slowly in the bottom of his stomach.

They reached the shed. There, Noah's flashlight caught from the shadows the sleek, taut fabric of an umbrella. It was lying in the wet grass, soaked and lonesome.

Clement stopped. He curled the fingers of both hands, his arms stiff at his sides. "Emmy?" he shouted. "Emmalee Rose! You come out here!"

The dark, ugly thing began to scrabble about in Noah's throat. He walked to the shed and pulled at the padlock. It was firmly clasped. He lowered the beam of the flashlight and saw where the mud had been churned by footsteps.

"Lord, she ain't never done me like this," said Clement. "Never in her life."

Noah swallowed. His whole mouth tasted of slick, putrid yellow. "Reckon I'm going up the hill to have a look."

"Well, now, that could be," said Clement. "She does like to go up there and visit with Miss Malathy some days. She ain't been in awhile, and I must say I've not been too neighborly myself of late. Though, Lord, what would possess her to head off there at this time of night I'm blamed if I could say."

Noah looked at the older man. There was an odd sharpness about the set of Noah's mouth and the look from his black eyes.

"She gets the strangest notions sometimes," said Clement. He spoke faster now. "I'd say you're right. That's where she's gone off. I'll run see about the folks inside a moment and grab my raincoat."

And so it was that, not long after, a slow, measured knock came upon Malathy Joan's front door. The knocking fell upon her head and scattered in her lap. She stirred. Her fingers twitched, and her shoulders shifted.

Someone called to her through the door. She raised her head, shaking to know the carpenter's voice. It claimed her as nothing else could. A numbness began to lift from her limbs. She saw a strong light outside her window, and she pushed her body so that her legs unfolded. She swayed onto her feet and moved towards the front door. The walls looked thin enough to walk through. The wind ruffled her gown and caught at her hair, and she breathed deeply. Then she gripped the doorknob and pried the door so the noise of rain swelled, and bright light burst upon her. She turned her head at once, and hair swept across her sight.

As she twisted away, Noah Carpenter glimpsed her face sudden and vivid before him, as the revelations of lightning when white branches tore upon the night and then were gone. The flashlight wavered in his hand. He let the beam fall towards the ground.

"Lord, Miss Malathy, honey," said Clement. "Did we go and wake you up?"

She stiffened and turned her head back towards them. Her eyes shone from the dark doorway. "You may have," she said. Her voice sounded like a rattle of sickness in her throat, and they could hardly hear what she spoke. Noah felt the breath drive hard into his chest. "I'm not sure myself," she said. "Why have you come to me?"

Noah looked at the bones coming like death through her face. He could not swallow. He knew no forgiveness in his soul for the hands that had made this happen.

"Emmy's wandered off in this rainstorm," he said. His fingers wrapped about the flashlight. "Has she been up here to see you?"

Malathy Joan leaned forward, one hand against the door facing, the other clutching her nightgown at the throat. "Emmy?" She looked all across Noah's face, and then she looked down at the boards beneath his feet. "I didn't see her," she said. "I haven't. I don't know where she might have gone," she said, raising eyes that asked and did not dare to believe. "Oh, God."

He liked nothing she said. He let the beam of the flashlight sweep across the boards. They were soaked and muddied. "I don't reckon the boy might have seen her," said Noah. "Is he asleep?"

Clement turned to Noah. "What do you mean? What boy?"

"A stray she took in," said Noah. He did not take his eyes from Malathy Joan. The look in them held no kindness.

Malathy Joan shook her head. "I told him to go," she said. "I don't know if he sleeps or where."

Noah stood and said nothing. The rain fell, and he listened to the cold sound.

"I would like to care what becomes of him, but it isn't in me," said Malathy Joan. She looked to Clement. "But Emmy, I don't know what's happened. You must tell me when she's found. Please."

"We'll do that," said Clement, nodding. "Sorry to bother you, Miss Malathy, but I sure had hoped she'd be here."

"It's no bother to me that you've come," said Malathy Joan. "I want her to be safe."

Noah hesitated. He edged his thumb against the flashlight switch. It moved a little but did not click the light away. "You might come down to the house," he said, then.

She placed her eyes fully before him. Her hands seemed weak and restless, and the sorrow in her eyes had no lack or end. "I don't think I can do that now. Noah. I'm sorry. Please," she said, lowering her eyes, "tell me that you've found her. I'll be here." She drew back, one arm crossed before her. She disappeared behind the door as it shut between them.

Without speaking, the two men turned from the house and headed down the porch steps. Then Clement said, slowly, "This night would make a fellow lose the hand on his arm. God knows where she's got to."

Noah nodded. He spoke carefully. "I reckon that's so." He pivoted his wrist so that the beam of the flashlight rippled across the slope. "And I reckon we'll know it, too."

The ground squashed beneath Noah's boots. The boy wandered somewhere, and he could be caught. Noah was satisfied of that. He figured the boy's hands were in much of this business, and he decided he would not be sorry to reckon with that miserable creature before it was done.

Only Noah Carpenter ever learned the fate of the young man who had lived for a time with the stranger woman in Jess Greenberry's house, and Noah never told what that was. On the night the young man disappeared, most of the townspeople had already fled to the lowlands, and the rest sat in Clement's living room and studied the two photographs displayed on top of the television set. It did not seem right to do otherwise, Veeny Anderson thought. In the black and white picture, a woman smiled prettily from a face that seemed as though it would rub out at the least scrubbing, a face far beyond earthly help now. But as Veeny looked at the second photograph, she could not help but pray. The girl there was full of color, with fresh, dewy eyes in a soft meadow of a face. It was the image that Clement saw as he climbed the rugged hillsides and called his daughter's name. It was the way Noah pictured the girl as he edged down the slopes towards the creek bed. It would be best to find her there in the yellow light of her home, he thought, than to find her where he walked. The dark of the sky was lifting, and the morning crept out grey and sullen. The creek waters roiled and churned below him. Pieces of the mountains rushed along with the frothing current, tree limbs and dead grass and old tires. They would be washed clean out to the Gulf of Mexico, maybe, and Noah wondered how many days and nights they would travel. He saw where the brown water spewed up against a great, slick, jumbled rocky mound. Then at the edge of his sight, he saw a large limb careening down the stream towards him, towards the pile of rocks, and he glimpsed movement along the tree branch. He saw a hand, an arm, grabbing hold.

Noah rushed towards the edge of the water, close to the place where the rocks heaped and jutted into the creek. Rain pelted through his clothes to his skin. The stout branch whacked against the rocks and lodged there, though the limb continued to jounce and shake with the force of the water. It seemed likely to give way again at any moment.

The figure that clung to the wood bobbed and turned about. Water threw the whole of its angry power against the person, as an arm lifted weakly and reached towards the bank. The fingers could barely touch the sharp, glittering surface of the stones.

"Here!" Noah shouted.

It might be Emmy Foster, needing his help, but it was sure some hapless soul who struggled in the flood. Noah stepped onto the outcropping. Everywhere he looked, the creek snarled about him, gnashing at the jagged edges of the rocks. He crouched, his hands gripping the wet, contrary surfaces, and went forward on his knees. The wind whipped at his rain slicker. He crawled near enough to see the head, the long, pale hair, the face uplifted like the hand. The blue eyes knew him at once.

"Carpenter!" the young man shouted. "Mr. Carpenter!"

Noah stopped, balancing himself on the rock. It was Addison who stretched fingers from the violent water. Noah did not feel his own hands and feet now at all.

Every line of the young man's face was wide and pleading. But the eyes looked calmly up at Noah, and even now, Noah mistrusted the cool look in them. He had reckoned from the beginning that this boy had lived lives enough, and there was not a decent one among them. His heart began to beat in a strange, strained rhythm. He did not know what foul thing clawed his throat, but he knew he had never hated a soul so powerfully before in his life.

"Mr. Carpenter!" Addison wriggled his hand. "For the love of God, help me!"

Noah felt the muscles in his neck and shoulders turn to stone. He could not bring himself to move. Twisting his lips, he thought what had been delivered into his hands.

Addison gritted his teeth. His eyes burned. "Look at you! How are you any better than I?" he cried. He fumbled his fingers towards the rock, his arm shaking. "Answer me!"

Noah knew absolutely the answer he would give, and it was the worst he had ever thought. Slowly, he leaned his weight onto his heels, edging away. He kept his arms at his sides. The rain beat across his back. Water trickled from his forehead. His face was as closed as a fist.

The boy shouted and strove against the flood. Kneeling, Noah watched and never moved until the branch tore loose from the rock at last and hurtled down the creek. The limb pitched about, and the young man's figure slipped below the water. Noah never saw him rise again.

Noah closed his eyes and lowered his head. His brow was hot, and the palms of his hands oozed. He knew what he had done. The breath squeezed into his lungs and out again. He knew there was no help for it in that world or the world to come. He knew that other eyes had watched, and his judgment was prepared. Three days later, when he learned that Emmy Foster's body had been pulled from the creek, he gripped the brim of his hat and pressed his lips together. He felt no more justified.

V

The rain clouds broke free from their moorings and drifted out towards North Carolina and the sea. In their wake, the colors of the world opened as on the first morning that ever dawned. The waters soaked into the ground, and dry land appeared again. Uncertainly, the people of Beulah Creek returned to their town. They drove up the road in their shining automobiles and came to the place they expected. There they sat in their cars and shut off the engines. They reached for the nearest hand. They bowed their heads. Judy Hendrick covered her face and cried. They had never witnessed such desolation in all their days.

Mud filled their rooms. Carpets sloshed. Houses stank. Veeny Anderson pulled on rubber gloves and picked Coke cans and empty detergent bottles from her flower beds. Jack Hendrick swept out the store, scrubbing, tossing away sodden boxes of food. Some folks simply held their hands up to heaven, for they could do nothing more. Betty McGuire's trailer had washed all the way to Sweet Haven, some ten miles down the road. The creek had even robbed graves from the cemetery by the Beulah Creek Baptist Church. Ruth Foster's grave was one of the desecrated.

As terrible a ruin as the flood had brought, the townspeople of Beulah Creek received their work and determined to bear it. The worst lot had not fallen to them.

None could look in the face of Clement Foster. He walked with stooped shoulders and a limp from a catch in his back. A team of strange men had come to Beulah Creek to find his daughter, and they found her come to harbor at the creek's edge. She was bunched together with plastic pop bottles and grocery bags that floated there, stirring as the water stirred. She lay face down, her chestnut hair trailing like knotted seaweed. Folks shook their heads as they spoke haltingly of this last detail and balked at the image of her death, fanciful and grotesque. While they cleaned and built and painted, the memory of what they had never seen, the body of Emmy Foster pulled from the creek, surfaced to trouble them. It caused them to speak more softly to one another at supper. It compelled Sarah Mullins to hug her daughters and kiss their foreheads. It sent Grandma Barnes to take meals up to Clement and sit with him awhile, knitting.

The word of Emmy's death had come to Noah Carpenter as he searched for the lost child. He lowered his head and gripped his hat with unwashed hands. His forehead ran with sweat. The things he saw when he closed his eyes seared his mind and burned his throat. He had believed her dead, and it was true. He found his hands useless once more. Slowly, he turned and walked back into town. He walked across the bridge that spanned the creek and climbed the hill toward the Greenberry place. As he climbed, his throat grew tight, for he could not stop thinking. He wondered if Malathy Joan waited in the rocking chair, her hands folded together. He wondered if he meant her to weep. He could not count the piles of ruin that blocked the way between them.

He came at last to the house and stepped onto the porch. His boots sounded loud in that dead land, where the grass was thin and brown and the color gone from the sky. He lifted his hand to knock, but the door jerked open. She stood before him gaunt and grim, with hardly skin enough to cover her. She shielded her eyes with her hand. They held a strange, pale light. She drew breath to speak, looking into his face, and all at once the light in her eyes went out.

"She's dead," said Malathy Joan. "Isn't she?"

Noah held to his hat. He nodded once.

She looked away, blinking as though to clear her sight. "Thank you," she whispered. Before he could figure what to say, the door closed once more, and he found himself leaning forward, listening.

"Malathy?" he said. He waited, turning his hat about in his hands. "Miss Malathy?" But she did not come back. The beat of his heart was not easy, and the motion of his blood unsteadied him. He did not like to trouble her further. Neither did he like to leave. He could have stood her grief better than her silence. Reluctantly, he turned from her door and walked through her yard, wondering if he had cause to give another answer.

Inside the Greenberry house, Malathy Joan leaned her back against the door. The breath entered her in short, sobbing bursts. She put the palms of her hands over her eyes, but she could not shut out the face that followed her. It seemed Emmy's gentle, simple face, but then it was Jess's face, marred by the eyes that shrieked from it forever. She sank down and squatted in the floor. She placed her fists together upon her breastbone and bowed her head. She had planted nothing in Beulah Creek but thorns and brambles. She had reaped only bitter fruit, dried pods that cracked open like bleeding lips. She cursed the house and the hands that first had built it. She cursed her own, true name. She let the shadows of the room trace across her for many days. The remnants of her last dinner sat in the oven, scorched to ashes a week cold.

Then one day, she heard the rocking chair creak. She lifted her head and looked through the straggling mass of her hair. She saw Jess Greenberry rise from the chair with cold and bleakness in the movement of her body. The spirit woman lifted her hand and pulled the pins from her chestnut hair. It fell in its lushness down her back, but her face was barren as the rock cliffs of the mountains. Jess's eyes moved aside once, to look where Malathy Joan crouched before the front door.

And then it seemed to Malathy Joan that she herself was standing, and that she saw the room through the eyes of the spirit woman, though Jess Greenberry walked beside her. Her feet carried her slowly across the floor. She felt herself lost and bereft and beyond the reach of any fingers but her own. All those years ago, she deeply knew, Jess had gone the same way. The room looked other than what Malathy recognized, the furniture of it shifted in her mind. Her thoughts glided like gibbering ghosts. She crossed into the kitchen and did not know how the rope came into her hand, but she knew it was the only right she could make, to make an end of her wretchedness. In that way, the will of Jess Greenberry was worked out at last in the life of Malathy Joan. Living the very secret she had sought, the stranger woman climbed onto the kitchen table and secured the rope to the rafter above.

That very morning, Noah Carpenter knew only that he did not find her thin and solemn face among the others when he raised his eyes. He did not like it, that she was not there. The people of Beulah Creek had gathered at a gaping place in the ground. The casket held the body of Emmy Foster, and the gravestone bore the name of Emmalee Rose, who had died before her sixteenth birthday. The air was warm and sweet, and a mockingbird sang from the roof of the church house. Clement stood near, his crumpled face hanging low, his eyes fixed in a grey place where no one else could come.

Noah shifted in his suit. He clenched his fingers like he meant to grab onto something. The mountains could crumble to gravel and creek beds revolutionize their courses, but nothing on earth could do away with the fact of Emmy Foster going into the cold, stony ground. Not even the freeing of her body on the last day could change it.

"It's a hard thing to know it's true," Clement had said to him three nights ago. The older man had stood before the window and reached out his arms to grip the molding on either side of the glass. "I wish I could say I know what's left," said Clement, "the blessed Lord and all. But the truth is, I'd rather have her back. I'd rather have her and her mother both." Noah had stood silent while Clement gulped and shook, and the girl's orange cat, Pumpkin, had looked up like a lost creature at each of them. "That may not be right of me," Clement said at last, his breath catching in his throat, "but it's how it is."

Standing there in the graveyard, Noah remembered, his hands empty at his sides. He did not look at the folks about him, for he did not like to pry into the faces of the grieving. Instead, his eyes took in the fine, strong spread of tree branches above the roof of the church, against the immense blue of the sky. It had been long since he had thought to look at such things. But he felt a tremor at the back of his neck as he turned last night's dream about in his mind. In the dream, he had entered a dark place, close and smothering, and had put out his hands to find his way. He could dimly see a high table at the far end of the room, and upon it was the candlestick he had made, standing at the very edge. Noah recalled what he had seen, and his heart moved faster. All about him, faces turned towards the ground and the great hole that was there, and that, too, was something to reckon. It was wrong that Malathy Joan did not come.

Looking at the curve of bough overhead, he knew then that he would have to go to her. He wanted some answers himself maybe. Around him, the people of Beulah Creek glimpsed the rigid brow and jaw of the carpenter and thought him fierce to see.

When the graveside service ended, Noah went to his house and put on his overalls and boots. He laid the palms of his hands against the smooth shape of the candlestick, and his hands were steadied. Then he turned and left the house, walking with purpose in the set of his shoulders. He walked more swiftly than any in Beulah Creek had seen him move. Veeny Anderson looked up as she swept her front stoop, and she opened her mouth with no noise. Grandma Barnes stood behind a window and narrowed her eyes as Noah passed. Sam McGuire spat, hooking a thumb through his belt loop where he leaned in the doorway. Noah walked with his face forward and his mouth placed in a dangerous line. He figured to see her and reach her if he had to pull the house down with his own two hands.

He headed up the hill. Clouds drifted across the sun. He heard the rattle of insects and the clear-throated whistle of birds. He could feel the weathered house crawling down the hill towards him. The air pressed so that he slowed his steps and drew an arm across his forehead to keep the burning salt from his eyes. He crossed the barren space where the garden had thrived. He climbed to the porch and knocked on the door. The sound broke upon the stillness. He called to her and leaned his head close to listen for her voice in reply.

Beyond the door, Malathy Joan stood barefoot on the kitchen table, the noose about her neck. She heard her name and the voice that spoke it. She turned her head in a loose movement and swayed a little, her legs no longer strong. Wherever she turned, she saw Jess Greenberry's chilling face, and the sight of it tightened her own fingers upon the harsh fibers of the rope. She would atone for the life she had made, for her vain belief that she could reach for other souls and try to love them. Her life was all she had left to give. But Malathy Joan also recognized who called to her through the door, and she trembled, hesitating. Through the smell of lilacs, she sensed she might want to be found, standing just as she was. She pressed her eyelashes against the flesh of her cheeks. She had once very much wanted to live.

Noah knocked again. Again, he called, "Malathy? Miss Malathy?" He waited for her voice and heard only the sound of his life rushing through his body. "Malathy Joan?" He beat the palm of his hand against the door. She did not come to answer.

He did not like what he was thinking. An icy pain pressed against his lungs. He had waited too long. All that time ago, he had walked from her and never returned to her. He did not dare to wait anymore.

He heaved his full weight and his strength into the door to break it open. It seemed to push back at him.

"For God's sake," he said, and tried once, twice more, to get through the door. It did not move. But neither would he.

He went to the front window to peer in and see her, to make another way in to reach her. He was startled instead by another woman's face in the window, with pursed lips and hair well-placed in a trim knot upon her head. Only the eyes looked unnatural, with their cold, eternal stare. He drew breath and realized he was seeing Jess Greenberry.

He kept his clenched hands lowered. He nodded to her. He knew nothing of dealing with spirits. But she had been a living human creature once, and he figured he could speak the name of the Lord against any danger. He met her look steadily.

"Mrs. Greenberry, I mean to come in there, with the Lord's help, if not yours," he said.

He could not tell the meaning of what she did then. She tipped her head to one side, and the whole of her face grew soft and blurred, as though the fall of rain smeared the glass. She lowered her eyes, and then she was gone.

He had raised his fist to break the window when he heard a clicking sound from the doorway. He turned and saw the door cracked open. He went to it at once, pushing it wider. He entered the front room. "Malathy?" he called.

The house smelled dusty and unused, as though the rooms had not been opened to light or air for many weeks. He looked where her purple shawl lay crumpled in the floor. Then, through the kitchen doorway, he could see Malathy Joan standing on the kitchen table in her nightgown. She seemed almost to be asleep, so quietly she stood. He stepped closer, not knowing what he saw, until he comprehended the rope about her neck, strung to the rafter overhead.

"Lord, don't!" he cried, and she stared at him. Noah reached out his hand. "Malathy, don't you move. Please. Be still."

Touching the rope, she waited with the last of her strength. But the act was sufficient. What had been before was forever severed from what could be. Jess had not waited in that time long gone, which inhabited Malathy Joan also right then.

With all his might, Noah ran towards Malathy Joan. He heard the beat and swish of his blood as he tore across the threshold into the kitchen. He saw her eyes close as if she gave up the ghost, and her knees caved, but Noah stretched out his arms, and he caught her as she began to fall. Struggling with the rope, he managed finally to slip it free from around her neck. He gathered her to him, holding her against his chest. She felt no more than a bundle of sticks to hold.

"I've got you," he said. Her hair fell all about her in disarray. He clutched her, discerning her breath, but reckoned he could lose her yet. "You're all right, I've got you," he said. "I'm taking you with me."

Noah moved to carry Malathy towards the back door, but Jess Greenberry was standing before it, her hand on the doorknob. He stopped and became very still. The ghost woman wore a long, dark dress. Her face was warm with color, her hair shining with a fresh, coppery hue. He had seen faces like hers in tinted photographs, impassive, unblinking, the sternness and regal bearing of mountain people imprinted as an everlasting testimony to the ones who came after them. He could look at them without flinching. He held hard to Malathy Joan.

"I aim to let you be," he said to the ghost woman. He spoke to her as though he had come to call on a Sunday afternoon, but his black eyes watched her carefully, and they were hard and sharp. "I don't figure to trouble you anymore, but I mean to pass by."

Jess Greenberry kept her left hand clutched against her skirt, the fingers folded. Now she lifted her fist and opened it palm upward. Something glittered there. The ghost held Malathy Joan's silver chain and pendant.

"I don't reckon you've got a right to that," Noah said.

Jess lifted one delicately arched eyebrow.

He shook his head. "You won't get nothing of mine in return," he said. He reckoned he knew better than to barter with a ghost woman. "You'll be let alone."

Jess curled up her fingers again, the necklace tight inside her fist. Noah's shoulders tightened. He felt Malathy Joan's breastbone rise and fall raggedly against him. He could not wait as long as Jess Greenberry could.

"Lady," he said. "Surely to God you know what it is to die."

Jess Greenberry stared at him. Her mouth faintly shook. She dropped her hand from the doorknob and began to walk towards him. He gripped Malathy Joan and braced himself against the cabinets. There was nothing else in the world for him to do. If he spoke against the ghost to ward her away, she might vanish with the chain and never return.

Jess Greenberry glided nearer, her lips turned low at the corners. Not an arm's length from Noah, she stopped. She lifted her fist. The silver chain and pendant dangled from her grasp. She gave a nod, the barest movement of her head upon her neck.

He swallowed. Watchful, he shifted his hand at the wrist and opened it.

Jess's fingers flicked apart, casting the chain into Noah's palm, and he closed his hand on the necklace. He began to breathe again. He drew back his hand until the silver touched Malathy Joan's arm.

"We'll go now and let you alone," he said to the ghost woman. "Maybe you can find some ease."

Jess Greenberry pursed her lips. A strange, wistful look came upon her face. She slipped aside. Noah went at once to the back door. He never turned his head. There was no sense in looking back. He turned the knob and dodged through the door. He found himself behind the house, clutching Malathy Joan. The bright day shone all around. The trees on Sumac Hill were sweet with birdsong and the scent of coming green. He turned to pass around the Greenberry house. He headed down the hill and reckoned himself alive.

It was not long before Noah Carpenter came down the slope by Clement Foster's house, carrying the long, slender, stranger woman in her white gown that ruffled and blew in the sunshine. The people in the town saw her bony limbs and the torrent of black hair, and they remembered her at last. They looked at the ruins of their homes and the garbage scattered in their yards. They looked where Noah Carpenter walked. One by one, they began to close their doors. Sam McGuire muttered and turned his back to the sight. Sarah Mullins grabbed Melinda's wrist and pulled her into the house. Judy Hendrick drew the living room curtains.

Grandma Barnes squinted from her window as Noah passed. She wrinkled up her mouth.

"Well, come on, dog," she sighed. She opened a deep drawer and took out her black bag. The dog lolled its tongue and stood up from the rug where it slept. Grandma Barnes stepped out her front door, the dog at her side, and followed where Noah had gone.

Noah carried Malathy Joan into his house and laid her on the bed. Her closed lids twitched some. She moved her hand fitfully, and she gasped to breathe. It hurt his throat to see her. Noah took the silver chain from his palm. He had carried it so tightly that the pendant had left its mark on the flesh of his hand. Now he leaned over her and carefully passed the chain about her neck. His fingers touched her hair as it spread upon the pillow. "Here," he said and wondered if she knew him. The clasp was small, but he fastened it and stood again to watch her. She grew still, and her breathing eased.

Something beat upon his door. Noah turned his head and listened. He would not open the door unless he had a good mind. But then he figured the sound could be the steady thump of Grandma Barnes's cane. He crossed quickly into the living room to look out the glass in the door.

When he saw the old woman in her purple polka-dot dress and black bowler hat with her black bag on her arm, he opened the door at once. Her dog sat back on its haunches and yawned. It kept its yellow eyes on Noah's face.

"She breathing yet?" Grandma Barnes pinched her mouth in a way that told her doubts.

Noah had a warning look in his dark eyes. It would make a trespasser fear. "I don't figure on her dying."

Grandma Barnes sniffed. "I reckon there's plenty you don't figure on." She stepped into the house without touching the hand that Noah offered to help her. "Show me where you've got her." The dog made no move to follow.

Noah brought Grandma Barnes to the bedroom where he had laid Malathy Joan. When they reached the doorway, they looked and stopped where they stood.

"Oh, mercy," said Grandma Barnes.

Malathy Joan sat bolt upright in the bed. She was trembling and breathing wildly, and her wide eyes watched where a dark, bloody mass spilled onto the sheets from between her legs.

Noah gripped the door facing. He was powerfully afraid.

Grandma Barnes turned and lifted her cane as though she would thrust the head of it into his chest. "Get," she said.

He saw the flicker in her squinting eye. He obeyed. He stepped back as she stepped into the bedroom, and she slammed the door. He stood there, not wanting to move, unwilling to wait without a thing for him to do. He went to the kitchen and began to wash the few dishes left from the morning. He had to occupy his hands somehow.

Not long after, Grandma Barnes opened the bedroom door. The sound brought Noah to the edge of the kitchen with the dishtowel in his hand.

"I need some warm water and a washrag," said Grandma Barnes. "I don't suppose you might have something else I could put on her."

So Noah filled a large bowl with water and fetched a washrag from the bathroom. "There's shirts in there," he said as he gave the things to Grandma Barnes.

"That'll do," said Grandma Barnes, and disappeared behind the door again. Noah walked slowly back to the kitchen sink and washed the dishes over.

A while later, the old woman stuck her head out once more. "Come here and help me with her while I get this mess of bedding off."

So Noah went and gathered Malathy Joan off the bed as she slept. He was not at all sorry to help. She felt warmer now, and her limbs did not hang as loosely as he held her. Grandma Barnes stripped the sheets and stretched clean bedding across the mattress. "You can put her back now," she said. "She'll do just as fine sleeping in the bed." He asked the old woman nothing, but laid Malathy Joan back down and returned to the kitchen. Grandma Barnes shut the door after him.

The third time Grandma Barnes came from the bedroom, she closed the door behind her. She walked to where Noah Carpenter stood with his hands in the dishwater. She set her black bag on the table. Noah glanced at her, still holding his coffee cup and the dishrag.

"Well," said Grandma Barnes. She cocked her head. The eyes in her tough, wrinkled face missed nothing as she watched him. "She may mend. That'll be for her to choose. But she's lost that baby."

Water began to ooze from the dishrag in his fist. Noah looked at Grandma Barnes until she thought he would look the flesh right off her face. She started to turn away from the hard things she saw there, but he turned first from her. He moved as though his arms were stiff and his feet were sore. He turned again to the sink and the dishwater. The old teapot-shaped clock ticked upon the wall.

"I reckon it's better so," said Grandma Barnes. She had told evil news enough in her long life. She could still see the skin about Jess Greenberry's eyes turn white and her lips go grey as Hazel had told that woman what she witnessed, crouching behind a tree in the early morning. "The Lord knows best," she added.

Noah lowered his head. He clutched the coffee cup in both hands. He moved his thumb about the curve of the handle. "I'm obliged to you coming," he said, very low.

Grandma Barnes picked up her bag. "Folks around here don't take too kindly to her these days. Want me to leave you the dog?"

Noah shook his head.

"Well, then," she said. "I'll get back."

He listened as she thumped to the front door. The dog barked as the door opened, and then the sound was shut away.

Noah put the coffee cup and dishrag into the water. He watched the places where they went down. The water at the surface seemed still, untouched. He had watched the boy sink into the water and drown in that way. He stood and held to the counter. Drawing a long breath, he lifted his head. Then he turned and walked to the bedroom. His boots sounded firm against the wooden floor.

Noah eased the door open and looked where Malathy Joan slept. Her chest moved as she lived. The covers were drawn up to her waist, and her hair fell down her like a rich garment. Grandma Barnes had opened his Bible and placed it, face down, upon her heart. He could see the bones of her face too much, and he hesitated to look at them too closely. She lay upon her back, and her right arm was lifted towards the slender line of her mouth, the hand curved at the wrist. He thought Malathy Joan a handsome woman. She had lived as seemed good and right to her, and the works of her hands were generously meant. In the end, he did not see her any other way.

He came into the room and drew a chair near to the bed. The wooden shutters were open in the room, and the pattern of sunlight shifted across her body. If she took no more thought of him, he would still be satisfied of her breath and her presence. He reckoned he could not help how he was made. Her candlestick rested upon the nightstand. He settled back in the chair to watch as she rested. He would be there when she woke.

VI

As morning moved over the mountains, Malathy Joan's hand shifted upon the covers. Her fingers slipped across the leather-bound Bible and touched the pendant that hung from her neck. Her brows drew closer together. Her forefinger traced the silver circle and the crossbars within. Her large eyes opened. She gazed at the strange ceiling. She tried to think where she found herself but could only recall shades like mountain ridges trailing mist, receding in the distance.

With effort, she rolled her head to look at the wall and the window with open shutters. Beyond the wall, the sky would soon be blue. She lifted her head, but the room paled, and she lay back once more against the pillow. Her chest moved. She felt the book rise and fall. She believed she should be thankful. Her eyes wanted to close again.

She turned her head towards her other side, and the breath caught in her ribs. Noah Carpenter sat in a straight-backed chair beside the bed. He slept stretched forward on his face, his head upon the mattress. A hot pain broke behind her breastbone and welled inside her throat. She had forgotten him and did not know how. There was a memory of hands that grabbed her. Her thin fingers brushed across the quilt as she moved her hand towards him. In the growing light, the colors in the quilt brightened like the quickening of petals in spring. She reached and touched Noah softly with her fingertips upon the crown of his head. She took back her hand before he should know.

She was sorry at once for what she had done. His breathing changed. He moved his head a little. Then his shoulders tensed, and he unfolded from the bed as though he had been called by name. He sat back in the chair, a hand to his neck, and regarded her with the same hard, quiet face she had always seen. The cut of his mouth was stern and even tended towards ugliness. She kept silent. He said nothing. His eyes seemed always set against whatever he beheld.

He lowered his hand. At last, he said, slowly, "It didn't seem right to me anymore to let you alone. Maybe you think otherwise."

She turned her head from side to side. "I believe whatever you could mean by coming," she said. "Thank you."

He nodded once. "It's good to have a sight of you again," he said.

She closed her eyes. She caught a lingering scent of lilacs, sharply sweet, and her heart grew sad. She fingered the silver pendant. "How did this come back to me?"

"It's no matter now," he said. "I mean you to mend."

She winced. "I suppose I will."

He was quiet then, and she began to think of sleep. She did not fear anything that might come to her in that place.

"Can I do something for you?" he asked, in a low voice that seemed almost tender.

She felt herself drifting. She would take with her the knowledge that the same walls held them both. "I don't think there's anything I can ask of you," she whispered. She placed her hands on the book that covered her chest and passed into a peaceful sleep.

So it was that Malathy Joan began to heal. She woke some hours later, thirsty. Noah came to her with a glass of water, a bowl of tomato soup, and a slice of toast.

"It's nothing like what you could fix," he said. "But there's plenty warming on the stove if you want it."

She felt strong enough to sit up against the pillow and feed herself. She was glad of the good, plain food. She ate two bowls full of the soup, and there was butter and honey for the toast, but nothing that she put into her could stop the hole in her heart.

She slept in the afternoon and woke for more food and water as night approached. She slept the night through until breakfast in the morning and then slept until dusk, when she awakened again. The chair by the bed was empty.

She sat up, still weak. A bitter cold ached in her ribs. She waited, and then she turned down the covers and swung her bare legs over the side of the bed. She would rather sit awhile, she thought, in another room. She held to the headboard and lowered her feet to the cold floor. It felt strange to go about with her legs uncovered. She huddled inside the flannel shirt she wore and tugged it towards her knees.

Carefully, she stood and felt herself light as wind in the trees. The room grew bright, and she closed her eyes for a time, but she managed to steady herself against the wood-paneled wall and make her way to the door. She crept through the doorway, clinging to the facing, and could see the living room before her. There was an old, sagging sofa, and beautiful wooden lamps with yellowed shades. The light they gave was low, but it warmed her to see it.

From the kitchen, Noah walked towards her, carrying a tray full of plates and glasses. He looked where she stood.

"Lord," he said and thrust the tray at the low table before the sofa. The sound of his boots on the floor came faster. "What are you needing?"

"I thought I'd sit awhile," she said. "I can't keep company with the dark tonight."

Noah thought her face looked too full of bones still and too empty of living. "Here," he said. "You won't fall." Her eyes seemed like the great night sky, glittering gold with other suns. He opened his hands.

He took hold of her, and they moved together to the sofa. Her legs trembled as though she were new born, and she was glad to sit and draw the heavy, dusty afghan over her knees. Noah walked over and turned on the little television set in the corner. He flipped the dial around, taking the picture through the four channels. He found a program with people laughing. He figured it was as harmless as most anything else he could find.

"That'll make a little racket anyhow," he said.

Malathy Joan nodded. Noah sat beside her on the sofa, and they ate their suppers from plates balanced in their laps. The television chattered, and they watched. In the space amid the noise like bright bubbles, they could be quiet for a time and think as they wished. Malathy Joan cradled the plate with her fingers and thought how this man fed her and ate with her, and yet she had betrayed both of them, herself not the least. She wondered why he had left her before and had saved her now. Her throat was dry and sour, and it was hard to swallow. She touched the silver at her neck.

Elsewhere, beyond the warm, dark wood and yellow light of Noah's house, others in Beulah Creek also watched. Inside their houses, they leaned towards one another across plates of pot roast or bowls of popcorn and whispered of evil things. They eyed the house of Noah Carpenter and noticed the flood had hardly touched it. Sarah Mullins and Betty McGuire both remembered they had witnessed Noah creeping about the town in the night. Bill Bledsoe said the carpenter had taken a sort of wooden staff with him. Though Jack Hendrick remarked loudly to his wife that folks had grown mighty dim-sighted lately, most everybody else believed that they had gone about blind for too long. They believed the stranger woman had sat high above them in a house possessed by demons, built upon poisoned land, and had let Jess Greenberry whisper to her of sins from years gone by. Some allowed that the flood was one of the stranger woman's works. Others declared that the flood was God's own judgment against the town for countenancing her presence among them. They had seen her borne down the hill in Noah's arms. They had seen her gown thin and white in the sun and wind, and her body insubstantial as clouds in winter. As they gathered in their homes to eat with one another, they paused with their glasses of iced tea halfway to their lips and muttered that she had already passed into the realm of spirits. They ought to cast her out from their midst. Moreover, they ought to set their faces against Noah Carpenter until he put that strange woman from him and turned from the path he walked. It was no less than the Lord commanded them.

That night, after Malathy Joan had lain out upon the bed and opened herself to sleep, Noah sat alone in the living room and fiddled with the newspaper. He went twice to the door when a knock came. The first visitor was Grandma Barnes. She wore a dark coat and had tied a black kerchief on her head. She gripped her cane with one gnarled hand and a shopping bag in the other.

"I can see she's better," said Grandma Barnes, when she had taken a look into Noah's face. She thrust the bag towards him. "Here's her things."

When Grandma Barnes had earlier gained sight of the Greenberry house, decrepit and decaying as it ought to have been long ago, she discovered Malathy Joan's clothing folded neatly on the stone step, her shoes laid out nearby, and the little wooden box nestled atop the garments. Thrusting herself onto the porch with her cane, the old woman had peered over the threshold into a quiet, broken place, smelling of damp and dirt and the long accumulation of years.

"I will say this," said Grandma Barnes to Noah, "I figure she done what she come for, though it's been a foolish, reckless business. That house has aged eighty years, if you can believe that. So maybe Jess has gone on her way. Though I don't suppose that's much to comfort Clement with."

More than ready to accept such a fate for the Greenberry house, Noah contended powerfully still with the death of Emmy Foster. "Miss Emmy dying is a hard thing to make out," said Noah, slowly, "without reason or justice. But surely she had some say in what she done, running off from home. Or else every one of the rest of us had a hand in what become of her, some way."

"Maybe. I reckon some had more to do with what's gone on than others," said Grandma Barnes. "Odd thing to me that boy's never turned up again."

Noah's face turned as still and hard and dark as Grandma Barnes had ever seen it look. She did not stay for his answer, because she did not need one. Death washed down Beulah Creek, and murder seeped through the mountains. It was the way of things, from everlasting to everlasting. She had the power of knowing it true. She turned and thumped away home.

The second visitor to Noah's house was Clement Foster. The grey hair at his temples had spread, and the skin seemed to have drawn up in folds at all the corners of his face.

"Lord, I didn't know she'd taken such a bad turn," said Clement. "Or I'd have come by before." He had seen Grandma Barnes carrying a sackful of things down from the Greenberry house and had taken to wondering. "It's a good thing you went up there to see about Miss Malathy," said Clement to Noah. Noah held the door open, but Clement shook his head. "If she's resting, I sure don't want to come bumping in and wake her," he said. He tugged at the drawstring of his jacket hood. "Just tell her I was by."

Noah nodded. "I'll do that."

Clement stepped back, his fidgeting hands suddenly still. "I reckon that's why she didn't come down, for Emmy. I wished I'd have thought it before."

Not until the third visitor dropped by the next morning, however, did Noah first hear what most in Beulah Creek had come to believe. He got up from the sofa where he had lain awake much of the night, listening. He pulled on his boots and headed to the wash room at the back of the house. He had stuffed a garbage bag full of the ruined bedding, and he meant to burn it that morning while she slept. As he leaned to take the bag from beside the washer, someone knocked at the back door. Jack Hendrick stood on the step, his hands in his pockets, looking uncomfortable.

"Morning, Noah," said Jack. "I was headed over to open up the store in a bit." He gestured with his head. "Can I come in and talk at you a moment?"

Jack's store was on the other end of town. Noah nodded. Jack stepped into the washroom, and Noah pushed the back door shut.

"You and Judy doing all right?" asked Noah.

"I reckon you can call it that," said Jack. "We're making do. Most folks are these days." He shifted on his feet as though his shoes pained him. "There's those that fall back on the Lord's mercy in hard times. Then there's those who take comfort in whatever kind of bad talk they can put their tongues on."

Noah said nothing. The line of his mouth tightened.

"It's fool things folks are saying," said Jack, scratching the back of his head. "But it's ugly, and I've spoken my mind against it. Nobody wills a flood to do folks harm, not the Lord or anyone else."

They heard a rustling coming along the hall and bare feet upon the cold floor. Noah turned towards the sound as Malathy Joan approached the doorway. Her face turned to them like a dying moon, hung from a violet sky above black mountains.

"Hello, Jack," she said. Her lips moved weakly at their edges. She kept the fingertips of her right hand towards the wall. Her legs were long and brown.

Jack could not believe the sight of her. "Good morning to you," he said. He stared at her face because he would not look anywhere else. He had not thought of her doe's legs. Ever after, he would see sometimes at twilight a shadow at the edge of the trees, darting away from him.

"You need anything?" Noah asked her.

She shook her head, and the edges of her mouth shifted again. "I can manage." She had tucked in the crook of her left arm one of the clean, folded garments that Grandma Barnes had brought down from the Greenberry house. Malathy turned and passed on down the hall. They heard a door close and not long after, the sound of running water.

Jack still watched the doorway and the empty hall. "I don't know what folks are aiming to do besides talk. But you'll hear whatever I know."

Noah's face did not move. "None of them are coming here."

Jack glanced at the carpenter. "No. I'd say not." He would not want to be one hunted by Noah's face in the dark of the moon, in the early morning before the sun.

After Jack left, Noah took the bag of bedding into the back yard. He spilled the things out upon the charred ground where other trash had burned. He set them on fire and stayed with them until they blackened and curled into nothingness. He pondered the whole while. Then he went back to the house with the empty garbage bag loose in his fingers.

As he stepped through the back door into the wash room, he smelled bacon frying. A frown came upon his face. He could not say why. It was a good smell, and he was hungry. He stood a moment and closed the door. Then he passed along the hallway to the kitchen, where Malathy Joan was scraping onions and peppers from a cutting board into a hissing skillet. She wore a long, grey dress with an intricate pattern of dark purple and had caught her damp hair back at the neck.

She set down the cutting board and glanced over her shoulder at him. Her lips lifted briefly at their corners. It was a grim smile. "Hello," she said.

Noah nodded. "You've been busy," he said. He saw how she steadied herself from time to time by pressing the palm of her hand against the countertop. He wadded the garbage bag and pushed it into the trashcan. He went over to the sink to wash his hands with yellow soap and dry them on the coarse towel hanging near. An answer to her came to mind, the thing he had promised Clement. He did not relish it any.

He opened the cabinets and took down plates and glasses for the table. She kept her eyes upon her work. She pressed the bacon flat against the pan with the tines of a fork.

"Clement Foster was by to see you last night," he said, walking to the table. "I told him I'd tell you so." He watched her. He would know what he saw.

Malathy Joan took her hand from the pan, and the fork clicked against the stovetop. She lifted her head. Her fingers found the silver pendant, and then she stood utterly still. All sounds stopped but the pop of grease in the pans. She shut her eyes.

"I loved her," she whispered. "God forgive me. I have been so wrong."

Noah looked where he curved his hand about the glass on the table. He himself had helped her hang doors in that house. He slipped his hand carefully, softly, over the mouth of the glass.

"I reckon she knows how you grieve her," he said. His throat felt thick, and his tongue felt slow. He did not think his words much comfort.

Sorrow tore from her throat in gulps. She groped for the stove and oven knobs and turned them off. She covered her face.

"Emmy," she sobbed. "Oh, Emmy." Water spilled into her hands and dripped down her wrists.

Noah loosed the glass. He heard the choke of her breath, and it broke him open to hear. Splinters and jagged edges buried deep within him. He walked behind her. Her thin, bony shoulders were trembling. He wanted to hold her like nothing he had ever wanted in all his life. Instead, he rested his hand upon her shoulder, and she cried harder. She took a hand from her face and held hard to his hand. He did not tell her not to cry.

They stood that way a long time. At last, she found a dry place within her, and her shaking slowly stopped. Her back stiffened, and her head came up. He took his fingers away.

She looked at the charred bacon in its yellow grease like bile and gestured towards the stove. "I have ruined all of this," she said, her voice still wet. "I'm sorry, Noah."

Noah shrugged. It could not be helped now. He fished the mixing bowl from the sink and poured out the water. He handed it to her. "You can throw out the scraps if you want," he said, not unkindly. "Some creature will be glad of it, I reckon."

She took the bowl. She could not look at him. She did not want to see what was not there, the good, kind, deep faith she had lost.

They ate oatmeal for breakfast, and then Noah went out to work in his shop. Malathy Joan cleared the table and washed the dishes slowly. She felt tired and unsteady. She tossed out the scraps and sat afterwards in the living room. She thumbed through an old grammar school reader and an ancient, battered copy of a book called *Angel Unaware* that she found tucked away on a shelf. She felt a chill within her chest as she remembered how she had wrapped her arms about the soft, fragile girl who had believed in her and loved her. She reached now and clasped the pendant instead, and that was how she pulled the breath once more into her body.

The sound of the clock counting on the wall did not rest her. She returned to the kitchen and poured a glass of iced tea. She carried it out to Noah where he fitted fresh-cut boards together. He looked hard at her before he came and took the glass from her fingers. She smelled clean, raw wood and the sweat of his neck and forehead as he stopped before her. Her chest pinched, but she did not move her face when he turned away. She would let him alone.

She left the workshop. The sunlight filled her eyes, and she shielded them with her arm. She was passing over the worn spot in the yard to the back door, when suddenly, she felt something small and hard strike her left shoulder. The pain took her breath. She grabbed the hurting place, as the stone thudded to the ground.

She looked where a young boy straddled a tree limb beyond the neighbor's fence. The boy grinned. The ache beneath her fingers sank deep.

"Go on!" piped a small voice. She could not see the child who spoke from behind the fence.

The boy drew back his hand, and she snatched up her skirts and hurried towards the door. A fistful of acorns pelted her shoulder blades. She heard the child squeal as she darted up the step. She flung open the door and pressed it shut behind her. She leaned back, her heart still running. Her shoulder grew tender and purple beneath her sleeve. It had come to this, that no one in Beulah

Creek would take her any more for a neighbor. She knew as surely as she had known the Greenberry house had waited for her. Her work there was done.

Noah was not slow to follow her. He found her in the living room. She stood before the large front window. Her hair fell like a thick cloak down her back, and her eyes were vast and dark. He thought she looked farther from him than she had ever been.

"You can tell me what happened," he said. "Because I won't have such happen again."

She shook her head. She gazed towards the high slopes that climbed toward Sumac Hill. "There's no life for me here anymore," she said.

He stood in a house that might as well be empty. He could not hold her. He could not let her go. He did not know what more he could do or say.

"A body's got to live how best they can," he said. "I reckon you know your own mind. But so help me, nothing will come to you while you're here."

She clasped the pendant. "I know."

He rested his hands at his sides. "When do you figure on going?"

Again, she shook her head. Her eyes turned slowly to take in his face. He thought of lights on the night ocean, and the great darkness beyond.

"I have been glad of you, Noah," she said. "I should like to have been a better neighbor. I didn't come to bring trouble, but it followed me all the same. I disbelieved you once. That was a great mistake."

He regarded her intently. "I don't reckon friends and neighbors need always be of a mind," he said.

Malathy Joan was quiet. "No," she said, finally. "There's no need to speak or listen then."

"That house has gone to ruin," said Noah. "Mrs. Greenberry's likely gone away with it. That's something you ought to know."

"Yes. I've done plenty here," said Malathy Joan. She remembered Jess, etchings of silver and lilac in her soul, had a swift notion she had stood with the lost woman at a dark and fateful moment. She lowered her eyes and spread her fingers carefully across her left shoulder. "Please don't trouble about this," she said. "That boy knows only what he's been told." She walked to the sofa.

Noah lowered his chin. "Well," he said. "I'll get back and work awhile yet. If anything like that happens anymore, you can tell me."

She gathered her skirts as she sat upon the sofa. "Yes. I can." Her eyes rested again on the candlestick that stood on the table. She reached and cupped her hand upon the dark curve of the wood. "You do good work," she said.

He did not know if he thought so still. He had walked through the town of Beulah Creek before she came, but could not see the town the same way any longer.

"I meant it for you," he said.

Malathy Joan looked at him then, the flick of her eyes swift and sudden. His face was a ridge that could not be crossed.

Noah turned to walk from the room. "You can take it with you when you go," he said. He knew then what he pondered in his heart. He did not mean to live anymore where he knew what everyone had done. He did not mean to die in his grandparents' house.

That night, Noah Carpenter sat late in the darkened living room. The television haunted its corner, reflecting the things around him small upon its screen. He realized he could not just pack them up to carry them with him. Some things would have to stay behind. He lay his head against the arm of the sofa. There were names and faces whose lives he knew. He knew, too, the trees that belonged to each piece of land. He could tell the passage of the sun as it trailed down the slopes each morning, and he favored the sound of the creek as it washed through the deep blue of summer dark. It was as well with him, though, to be in the place where she breathed. He would need to know her mind.

He closed his eyes and opened them again at once. He heard an engine idling out on the road in front of his house. He put his feet to the floor and went to the front window.

It was Chad Mullins's truck, it looked like, and several shapes like people crouched in the bed. He reached his arm to the light switch by the front door, and the yard appeared and the faces of men in the truck bed. He could name every last one. The men shifted into the shadows. The truck drove on.

Noah stood long after the road was empty. He had caused a boy to die before now and could not say he was sorry for it. He did not know if such a thought might come to him again.

He left the light alone and sat back on the sofa. Weariness came to his mind. After a long while of listening, he rested his head and shut his eyes. He stood all night upon the shore of a grey ocean and watched the waves break and roll to his feet. His ears only held the hiss and sigh of the sea.

Perhaps it was his dream that kept him from listening. He never knew how he did not hear Malathy Joan rise from her bed and pass down the hallway at the back of the house. The handles of the shopping bag looped upon her wrist. Her left hand clutched her shawl close about her neck. She carried the candlestick in her right hand. She stepped through the space that she opened between the back door and the house. She hastened through the grass that clung to her skirts and shoes, making them heavy and damp.

Then she slipped along the road that led from Beulah Creek. She traveled in the early morning, when the land lay brown and grey and black, and vapors crept like fingers down the mountains. She passed places wracked and emptied by the flood, witnessed the starts of new homes. She passed the house of Grandma Barnes, who saw her and thought Jess Greenberry was not the only lost soul to have walked the earth. Malathy Joan moved among the buildings of the town and bore them with her, even as she herself lingered along the banks of Beulah Creek for all time.

Jack Hendrick was taking some Windex to the front door of the gas and grocery when he saw her long shape beyond the glass. She moved quickly, her skirts like the stirring of summer trees, her hair billowing, a gathering of stormclouds to come. Jack set the bottle right down. His heart beat so hard that he thought it would bruise against his ribs. He could only watch her go, but there was no question of what he would do besides. He scrambled behind the counter and grabbed twice at the telephone.

The sound of ringing was the first that Noah knew that morning. He frowned and lifted his head. He had slept wrong and was sore for it. Slowly, he got to his feet. He crossed to the telephone that hung on the wall near the kitchen door and answered.

"She's gone," said Jack.

Noah braced his hand against the wall. It did no good.

"I just saw her go," said Jack.

He knew what Jack was saying.

"For God's sake," said Jack. "You just going to let her?"

"I appreciate you called," said Noah. He hung up the telephone.

He did not know how long he pushed against the wall. He raised his head at last. He went to the bedroom door. He opened it and looked at the bed neatly made, without wrinkle or blemish.

The sight of it made him move. He went through the house and then through his workshop. He gathered up what he could carry and loaded the things in the back of his van. He locked all the doors to the buildings and threw his hat into the front passenger seat. He would not be there again. He knew that the man who set on his way and then looked behind him was not fit for the kingdom or anything else. He drove out to Jack's store, and Jack came to the van. Noah thrust the house and shop keys out the window.

"I'd rather you kept an eye on things, if you could," he said. "I don't figure on using those."

"I'll do it," said Jack, nodding. He took the keys.

The people of Beulah Creek ran to their doors. They watched the van dwindle down the road with the dark that melted from the mountains. They knew the van had gone into the lowlands and was lost to them. Some walked up the road and stared at the carpenter's house. It was more than they could believe. They decided that Noah Carpenter would drive his van to the ends of the earth, but that he would never again find the slender, ghostly, dark-eyed stranger woman. They told it for the end of the tale ever after, for they knew nothing more.

But it happened that Malathy Joan walked along the road, and she walked with a sadness unlike any other she had befriended. When she heard the van approach her from behind, she slowed, but walked on, the candlestick pressed against her body. The van stopped. She heard the door open and then Noah's boots coming after her, clipped and brisk. She kept walking just the same.

Noah crossed the space between them. He reached and caught her arm, and she gasped as he pulled her around to face him. He saw her eyes stricken, her lips opened. He turned her loose.

"I've got no cause to hold you," he said. "But I need to know your mind."

She blinked. "I waited for you," she said. "All the time I was in Beulah Creek I hoped. I never did know your mind, Noah. And then I did not believe you were coming back." The turn of her mouth was sorrowful. "I missed you."

He would not turn aside, to the right or to the left, for anything on earth. "That boy wasn't the only one to do wrong by you," he said. "God knows. But you would go and not speak. I can't let that be."

She furrowed her brows. "What would you have me say?" She kept the candlestick tight against her chest. "I have wronged you every way. I can't wait for what won't happen. I am going away."

The set of his mouth was firm. "I can't let you go," he said.

"I can't ask you to come," she said. "There is death wherever I go." Her eyes trembled. "It touches everything I touch."

He could not believe such a thing. He hesitated. Then he stretched out his hand and laid it against the side of her face. She shut her eyes. "I would cleave to you," he said.

Her throat tightened. She drew a shuddering breath and looked at him again. "I would let you," she said.

He moved his thumb across the strong, fine bone. "There's a fishing place I know," he said. "It's back in the hills a ways. There's a shed there and a boat."

The gold in her eyes looked like morning. "I'll come with you," she said. "I would be glad to see that place with you."

Nobody in Beulah Creek ever knew that Malathy Joan and Noah Carpenter found one another. But Jack Hendrick looked always towards the front door of the gas and grocery when the bells jangled on their ropes. And in the mornings as he walked to the store, he looked down the road where they had gone, and he believed.

Acknowledgments

This novel began when I lived as a graduate student in Indiana in the mid to late 1990's, but the groundwork for it was laid even longer ago. Born into suburban Appalachia in the 1970's, I grew up listening to my father's music collection of folksingers and singer-songwriters—so it is no surprise that Joan Baez's cover of Bob Dylan's "Sad-Eyed Lady of the Lowlands" has exerted an obvious influence here. But I also spent huge swaths of my childhood roving pastures and walking railroad tracks in Union and Rhea Counties in eastern Tennessee, at a time when the working Appalachian family farm was entering its sad decline. Those foundational experiences, too, have found their way into my writing. This novel was one way I had—as an Internet-using, interstate-traveling, fast-food-eating Appalachian—of exploring the quintessential, mythic mountain legacy of log cabins and barbed-wire fences, fiddle tunes and family graveyards. An heir to that legacy, I still engage and wrestle with its hold on me.

The first two chapters of this work—in slightly different form and under a different title—placed first in the 2001 Tennessee Writers Alliance Novel Competition, awarded at the Southern Festival of Books in Nashville, Tennessee. The initial draft of the novel was only half-written at the time—many thanks to the judges for their early encouragement.

In the early 2000's, readers of the finished first draft offered many helpful suggestions. They include Silas House, Monica Eiland, Melissa Kleiner, and though by now, they have probably forgotten what they said, I appreciate their input more than they know. Other friends and family members read the manuscript through revisions of later years. A great big thank you goes to Mandy Branch, Peggy Green, Robin Hembree, Doris Henderlight, Tracy Henderlight,

Andrew Hutsell, Linda Hutsell, Lisa McMasters, and Becky Szymanski for taking time to provide your valuable feedback.

I owe an enormous debt of gratitude to the members of my writing group—Robert Beasley, Jeff Horner, Stephanie Levy, Nancy T. McGlasson, and Bonny Millard—whose in-depth critiques of every chapter made this into a much better book. Nancy and Bonny also took extra time from their busy lives and gave the manuscript additional readings during the final rewrites in 2014, and I am profoundly grateful to them both. Thank you, all my writing friends, so, so much for your comments and criticisms, your nurturance and support. This book would not be possible without you.

Special mention should be made of the Tennessee Mountain Writers' January Jumpstart session led by J.T. Ellison in 2014, which inaugurated the final rewrite of the book, and the Cumberland Gap Writers' Studio session led by Michael Chitwood in the summer of 2015, where participants reacted to the reading of the manuscript's opening pages. Big, deep thanks to Darnell Arnoult for her great kindness.

I am overwhelmed with thankfulness for Laura Still and Brent Minchey of Celtic Cat Publishing. Both their unshakeable belief in this project and their patience with me, the neophyte, during the production process have been boundless. I am honored that they have cared about my book so passionately and taken care of it so well. Thanks to Renee Kochis for coming to the rescue, to Nancy T. McGlasson for the early-morning photo shoot, and to Dorothy and Caesar Stair for the enormous gift of their hospitality.

Many, many people have encouraged and inspired me along the road I've traveled to get here. Writing teachers Carol McMurray, Gloria Oster, and Bland Simpson passed on their knowledge and wisdom. Writing communities embodied in the Appalachian Writers' Workshop in Hindman, Kentucky, in the Mountain Heritage Literary Festival in Harrogate, Tennessee, and in the Knoxville Writers' Guild welcomed me into their midst. Thanks to these and to others named and unnamed for giving of themselves—it has made a powerful difference to me.

Thanks to Fred and "Ms. Jane" for their kind affirmation, especially in the darkest of times. Thanks to Terri Parsons for going the distance with me—you are the real-life miracle worker who every day helps the dead to live again.

(And a shout-out here to Sherry Hutsell for always keeping me in line!)

Finally, love and gratitude to those who have walked alongside me the longest—Jane Hicks, my mentor and friend for decades who first showed me the ropes, and Will, Linda, and Andrew Hutsell, who have been through it all with me. This book is for you. There have been good times and there have been bad, but you have loved me no matter what. Thank you for not giving up. Thank you for being there. Thank you for believing in me.

About the Author

A native of Kingsport, Tennessee, Melanie K. Hutsell grew up listening to family stories of ghosts and tales of recalcitrant women. A life-transforming discovery from her childhood—that the lyrics to Peter, Paul, and Mary's song, "The Three Ravens," appear in a book of ballads—propelled her forever into the magic realm where literature, music, and folklore converge.

The first two chapters (in slightly altered form) of *The Dead Shall Rise* (then titled *Everlasting*), won first place in the Tennessee Writers Alliance Novel Competition in 2001, awarded at the Southern Festival of Books. Melanie's short fiction has appeared in *Appalachian Heritage, Still: The Journal* (www.stilljournal.net), *Trajectory*, and the Knoxville Writers' Guild anthology, *Outscape: Writings on Fences and Frontiers*. Her short story, "Celestial Images," was a Judge's Selection (as judged by Holly Goddard Jones) in the 2013 Literary Contests at *Still*. Melanie has also published poetry in *The Sow's Ear* and contributed to the *Encyclopedia of Folklore and Literature*, edited by Brown and Rosenberg.

Melanie holds a BA in English from the University of North Carolina at Chapel Hill and an MA in English from Indiana University at Bloomington. An avid reader and music lover, she currently lives in Maryville, Tennessee, in the foothills of the Smoky Mountains.

Made in United States
Orlando, FL
09 December 2023